I0687135

FRONT SWINE

The Russian Series
Book Three

Charles Whiting
writing as
Klaus Konrad

SAPERE
BOOKS

FRONT SWINE

Published by Sapere Books.

24 Trafalgar Road, Ilkley, LS29 8HH

saperebooks.com

ISBN: 978-0-85495-637-1

BOOK ONE: *GOING UP*

'They were men rudely torn away from the joys of life. Like any other men whom you take in the mass, they were ignorant and of narrow outlook, full of sound common-sense, disposed to be led and do as they were bid, enduring under hardship, long suffering ... but at intervals there were cries and dark shudders of humanity that issued from the silence and the shadows of their great human hearts.'

Henri Barbusse

CHAPTER 1

Snowflakes fell gently, almost sadly. In the snow outside the echoing station, pink-kneed boys from the Hitler Youth rattled their cans. As usual they were collecting for the 'Winter Relief'. Prostitutes stood in the dark doorways of bomb-shattered houses which surrounded the station, flashing their blue-covered torches to indicate they were waiting for business. Heavily-laden soldiers returning to the Front in the East trudged by miserably, hardly bothering to salute the waiting officers, accompanied by sobbing wives and girlfriends, and watched suspiciously by hard-eyed military policemen with carbines slung over their shoulders. At the front entrance of the station under the bold white banner proclaiming 'Wheels Roll For Victory', a middle-aged, cynic-eyed civilian in an ankle-length green-leather coat stood, watching everything. He had Gestapo written all over his lined, brutal face.

Colonel von Dietz, commander of the 69th Infantry Regiment, stamped his boots and said to his companion, 'Well, Pill, here we go again. Off to the Soviet workers' paradise.' He coughed and his breath went grey in the icy air, wreathing momentarily the harsh handsome face.

The Pill, otherwise known as Doctor Hartung, the 69th's MO, smiled up at the younger man. 'Off we go again, Horst,' he said, 'for the ... how many times have they sent us to Russia now? I forget.'

Von Dietz held up four fingers of his elegantly gloved hand. The first faint strains of the band could just be heard.

'Four times!' the Pill mused, stroking the straggly moustache which hid the mess a piece of Russian shrapnel had made of his upper lip the last time the 69th had gone out. 'As many as that, eh.' He sniffed. 'Like a damned sausage-meat machine, isn't it, Horst? We pump in good German lads at this end and they come out bloody bits of dead meat at the other end — in the East.'

Von Dietz gave him a faint grin. The music was getting louder. It would be the latest draft, he told himself. Soon they'd be in the smoke-filled warmth of the troop train which would carry them on the long journey to Russia and the Front.

'Mustn't say things like that, Pill,' he chided the other man mildly. 'If our friend from the Gestapo over there hears, he might well accuse you of defeatism. A serious crime in this year of Our Lord 1942 when anyone with any sense knows that final victory is just round the corner. At the moment we are simply incurring a few minor losses in Russia, a mere straightening of the line as the Gift Dwarf's papers have it.' He chuckled throatily.

'You're a cynic, Horst.'

'It's the only way I can prevent myself going mad, Pill,' von Dietz said, his voice suddenly grave. Then he barked, 'Sergeant-Major Bulle!'

'The Bull', as the 69th's Sergeant-Major was nicknamed behind his back, swung round, his cruelly muscled shoulders seeming about to burst from his field-grey tunic, his face brick-red and brutal under the too small steel helmet, '*Sir*!' he bellowed at the top of his voice making the Gestapo man under the banner glance at him in surprise.

'Ready the flag party — the draft's approaching, Sarnt-Major!'

'*Sir*!' The Bull swung round woodenly, as if his body was worked by rigid springs and bellowed at a handful of old soldiers, the light patches on their darned and faded uniforms indicating that they had all been NCOs at some time or other before being relieved of their rank. 'All right, you bunch of candy-cracks and piss-pansies, you heard the CO! Form up at once, or I'll have the vaseline to your slack arses in zero-comma-nothing-seconds!'

Unimpressed, the veteran survivors from the murderous blood-letting in Russia, shuffled into some semblance of military order as the strains of the Berlin Military Garrison Band grew ever louder.

'Wonder if any of them will have thought to have looted the wet canteen before they left, Rudi,' René Deltgen asked in Rhenish sing-song, remembering he had only one bottle of firewater left to last him the whole long journey to Popovland.

'A lot of wet-arsed greenbeaks *like that*!' Red Rudi said scornfully, his face as usual flushed an irate red. 'You know the kind of shitty cannon fodder the regiment gets these days? They wouldn't even know what sauce looks like!' He puffed out his skinny cheeks contemptuously. 'Mother's milk and sugar-titty is what that kind likes, you arse with ears.'

Deltgen grinned, in no way offended by his old-running-mate's outburst. Red Rudi was always surly, even now after he had spent a solid four days in bed with one of Berlin's most expensive pavement-pounders. 'Take a gander at the floor, ladies,' the two of them had joked, as they had parted to go to their bedrooms with the two whores, *'cos you won't be seeing nothing but the ceiling for the next four days!'*

'I thought you'd got all yer dirty water off'n yer chest, Rudi,' he said. 'What yer bitching about?'

'We're off to Popovland, aren't we?' Rudi grumbled as the band swung round the corner and the street thundered and reverberated with the martial music. 'That puts years on anybody.'

'All right, you slime-shitters!' the Bull's tremendous voice shattered into the two running-mates' conversation. 'No more talking in the ranks! Here they come!'

Eight abreast the band packed the avenue as they advanced on the station. At their head marched the majestic drum major, swinging his mace with imperial ease, his gaze fixed on a distant horizon, far from this miserable war-torn Berlin with its yellow-faced, half-starved civilians packing both sides of the street.

Behind came the draft — thin-faced young men in their teens, their skinny shoulders seeming too small for the great packs that bore down upon them, their uniforms new and ill-fitting.

'Christ,' Deltgen whispered out of the side of his mouth as he caught sight of their proud, scared faces for the first time, 'cast yer glassy orbs over those heroes, Rudi! A month in Popovland and the whole wet-tailed bunch o' them'll be looking at the potatoes from underneath.'

It was the same thought that was flashing through Colonel von Dietz's mind, as he raised his gloved hand to his cap in salute as rank after rank of soldiers began to march past, heads turned woodenly to the left. They were boys, mere boys, skinny and undernourished, the products of three years of severe rationing and the foul air of air-raid shelters. They had none of the red-faced beefy look of the men he had taken to war back in 1939. The barrel was obviously being scraped clean.

At his side, the Pill whispered, 'Bed-wetters to a man, I'll be bound, Horst.'

'Masturbators, too, Pill. Go on, say it,' von Dietz whispered back. 'Every second one of them flat-footed as well.'

The Pill grinned. 'Hammer-toes and hang-nails,' he said, as the band crashed to a halt and somewhat more raggedly the draft did the same.

'Hernia and piles,' von Dietz continued the litany of hopelessness with grim humour, as the young officer in charge of the draft ordered them round to face their new commanding officer and Red Rudi roughly unfurled the flag of the 69th, hung with the silken streamers of battle honours that went back to the days of 'Old Fritz' himself.

'Stomach ulcers as well,' the Pill added as the young officer strode towards them his face set in a look of youthful purposefulness. At ten paces, as regulations prescribed, he stopped, stamped his right boots down hard and cried in a shrill thin voice, his breath fogging the cold air, 'Ensign von Doerr, War Volunteer, and two hundred men of the Draft, all present and correct, *sir*!'

Von Dietz touched his cap to acknowledge the report. He did not know the young officer, but he knew of the family. An Ensign von Doerr had carried the flag of the Regiment at St Privat in 1870 and had been mortally wounded doing so; and if he weren't mistaken, there had been a Captain von Doerr with the Regiment at the Battle of the Nations back in 1814. 'Thank you, Ensign,' von Dietz said, a little pleased that his newest officer belonged to the tradition of the 69th. 'Please have your men…'

The sudden dry sharp crack of a single rifle-shot cut into his orders. To von Doerr's right, the massive drum-major clutched his shoulder, a look of absolute disbelief on his well-nourished face that this was happening to him, as blood started to seep through the fingers of his white-gloved hand. The mace clattered from his other hand. Slowly his knees started to buckle beneath him. For one long moment there was an awed silence, while the open-mouthed crowd and the shocked young soldiers stared at the sinking giant. He hit the ground with a thud.

The noise broke the spell. Women screamed. Von Doerr dropped to the ground, as the panic-stricken crowd scattered and up above them on the snowy roof the lone marksman raised his rifle once more. 'Get out of the way, he'll fire again!' they yelled, flinging themselves into the snow, piling into doorways, diving into the ruins, dragging their wailing children with them.

'*Liberty for the Jews*!' the lone man on the roof cried above the screams and yells. '*End the war in Russia*! *Depose the tyrant, Hitler*!' He fired again. The slug howled off the entrance to the station and on the ground Ensign von Doerr jerked visibly, while the Pill and von Dietz fumbled with their pistol holsters. The two helmeted chain dogs were quicker off the mark. Unslinging their carbines, they raised them and took quick aim. Slugs ricocheted off the brickwork of the chimney nearest the lone sniper as they pumped shot after shot upwards, striking up vicious little spurts of blue flame each time.

Suddenly aware of the danger the unknown man dropped his rifle. It clattered down the steep roof and went over the side. Frantically he began to crawl up the slippery slates. Bullets followed him, jetting white snow at his heels. Now he had almost reached the gable. In a minute he'd have it, lever himself upwards and over, out of range. But that wasn't to be. A bullet caught him squarely in the right shoulder. Von Dietz could hear audibly the thwack of steel smashing bone. The marksman screamed shrilly. His hands flailed the air, as if he were climbing the rungs of an invisible ladder. Desperately he tried to keep his balance. To no avail. In a flurry of snow he came sliding down the roof, hurtled over the side and hit the ground below like a sack of wet cement.

The two MPs and the fat Gestapo man immediately began to run towards the groaning man. The crowd surged forward. The Gestapo man shouted something and they drew back. Von Dietz could now see. He watched as the dying man tried to raise himself, as though about to cry out another of his treacherous slogans. He watched as the Gestapo man now towering above the dying sniper fumbled in the pocket of his leather-coat for his pistol. He found it. And then he casually placed the muzzle just below and to the right of the dying man's ear. He winked and grunted something to the watching chain dogs. Next instant he pulled the trigger. There was a muffled crack, a cry of fear from the watching crowd, and the sniper's head burst open and thick red gore, like the pulp of a split fig, started to ooze out of the shattered skull.

Without a second look at the man he had just murdered, the Gestapo man rose to his feet. The crowd drew back apprehensively as he started to make his way through them to where a shocked von Dietz stood with the Pill, while Ensign von Doerr still lay absurdly in the snow.

The Gestapo man touched his hand casually to the black felt hat which he wore pulled down low over his narrow forehead. 'It's all right, sir,' he said in a voice thickened by decades of cheap cigars and even cheaper schnaps. 'One of them communist shits... Lot of them about since we've been having a bit of a trouble in Russia.' He smiled suddenly, revealing a mouthful of gold teeth. ''Spect if he'd have gone where you and your brave lads are going, he'd have soon changed his mind about the Soviet paradise. But too late for that now, sir, isn't it?'

'Yes,' von Dietz replied automatically, too shocked by the sudden murder to react properly.

The Gestapo man nodded again. 'Well, sir, best of luck and give the Ivans a bit o' stick for me,' and with that he started to stroll back to his post.

'Thank you,' von Dietz said hollowly and then his gaze fell on a shame-faced von Doerr who was rising now and brushing the snow from his knees. 'For God's sake, man!' he bellowed in sudden anger — at what he didn't quite know. 'Get your damned men on the train and let's get out of this place! *At the double!*'

'Yes, sir ... of course, sir ... at the double, sir...' Flustered and crimson, von Doerr spun round on his men and started rapping out orders. Von Dietz stared at the still shape, sprawled in the snow, its shattered head now mercifully covered by one of the chain dogs' capes, 'I can't,' he began.

But the Pill caught him by the arm and said firmly, 'I know, Horst, I know. Berlin ... Germany, 1942...' Firmly he began to steer the younger man to the station and the waiting train, now packed with soldiers. All about them were the fading chalked slogans of the year of victories, *'Moscow, here we come!'* ... *'Stalin, you better watch out!'* 'We're better off at the Front...'

CHAPTER 2

Colonel von Dietz looked around the crowded, cluttered wagon, with its straw-covered floor, and raising his voice above the steel clatter of the train wheels, addressed his officers. '*Meine Herren*, now that we have crossed the frontier of the Reich, I can tell you our destination.'

The officers craned their necks, and the Pill at his position next to the glowing pot-bellied stove, with which he was honoured on account of his age and. seniority, puffed happily at his pipe. He had heard it all before; still he enjoyed the traditional routine of 'going up'.

Colonel von Dietz smiled thinly. 'I think I can say it is not a particularly lethal area of the Eastern Front. The air won't be too filled with lead, you'll be happy to hear.' For a moment his eyes fell on Ensign von Doerr and he noted the look of relief on the young officer's face. 'We're off to Leningrad.'

'*Leningrad*!' the officers exclaimed, some apparently disappointed, some obviously happy; for the Russian port was regarded generally as a quiet front.

'Yes, the place has been under siege now since autumn 1941. That means the poor Popov buggers have been holding out for over five hundred days. They tell me that they're so hungry that they boil the glue out of wallpaper to make food, and eat the fat they grease axles with too. Inside the city they're dying like flies. But still they hold on.' He tugged the end of his nose. It was very cold, but he hadn't the nerve to disturb the Pill so that he could get closer to the warmth of the glowing stove. 'So that's where we're going and although I am not in the Führer's confidence, a little bird has told me that no offensive against Leningrad is planned this winter.' He smiled at them. 'For the time being therefore, gentlemen, you will not be expected to die for Folk, Fatherland and Führer.' His officers returned his grin and Ensign von Doerr gave an audible sigh of relief. Suddenly von Dietz realized that the youngster was scared, very scared.

'Now that means positional warfare, the kind of trench fighting that the Pill there, who is, as everyone knows, a hundred years old can recollect from the First War.'

'Happy days,' the Pill said, taking his clay pipe out of his mouth. 'Now that was a real war. Since then they really have spoiled things up at the top.' He winked solemnly at a grinning von Dietz. 'Running around in tanks and aeroplanes and things. A fellow can't settle in anywhere these days at the Front.'

'Well, all the same,' von Dietz continued, his face hardening again, 'we shall have to take certain precautions. I will not have my regiment suffer casualties due to the carelessness of my officers.' His grey eyes flashed around the circle of expectant faces. 'Some of you have been out before. Most of you haven't. For the benefit of *all* of you, let me tell you of the routine of trench life and the precautions we must take once we're in position outside Leningrad. Stand-to is at dawn, and every officer on duty will ensure that his fields of fire, his stores, his men and his trenches are in order. After breakfast, two men out of every three are to be stood down while the remaining man stands sentry. The men on stand-down are to be employed under cover making repairs to duckboards, sandbags etc. They are not to be needlessly exposed. Is that understood?'

His officers, suddenly grave as they started to realize the new kind of life they were going to be exposed to, nodded.

'Rations will be brought up after dark and we will stand-to again at that time because Friend Ivan knows our routine as well as we do. That is a favourite time for him to attack.'

'Yes,' the Pill commented good-humouredly from the stove, 'they prefer our giddi-up goulash to that dried fish muck they eat. That's a good enough excuse for Friend Ivan to launch an attack, if he's fired up enough on proof-vodka.'

'Exactly,' von Dietz agreed and continued. 'Now apart from an attack from Friend Ivan, the only real dangers come from artillery bombardments and his snipers — they are fiendish. Now something can be done here, too, to prevent needless casualties. Here are some tips, which might save your own and your men's lives. So listen carefully and take it in.' At the stove, the smile vanished from the Pill's lined, wise face. He knew only too well how skilled the enemy snipers were; in his time he had treated more than enough of the casualties they had caused.

'Never put your head up above the parapet in the same spot twice. Move about at a smart pace. Don't stop until you're clear of the danger zone. Carry a rifle when you're in the line and not a revolver. Have it unslung and ready to fire at all times. Avoid concentrations of our own guns — they are prime targets for Friend Ivan. It's hard luck on the gunners, but,' von Dietz shrugged, 'my prime responsibility is the 69th. In short, be alert all the time and use the ground like a native would. Don't you agree, Pill?'

The MO nodded. 'Exactly, carelessness costs lives. Make sure, also, that your water-bottle is filled at all times when you're in the line. Snipers love water-spots — and latrines.' He smiled grimly. 'You'd be surprised if I told you how many officers I've treated who've been shot in the arse while they were sitting on the thunderbox.'

A rumble of laughter greeted the doctor's sally and he pointed his pipe at the officers, saying, 'Stay constipated and lousy while you're in the line. As soon as you get the shits and the felt-lice start to march off looking for another human blood donor, you can count yourself as good as dead.' He looked around their young inexperienced faces sombrely. 'Boys, they say Leningrad is an easy front, but believe this particular old head, you can get yourself killed dead *there* as well as anywhere else in the east. Mark my words.' With that he sat back against the stove and began to puff his clay pipe stolidly, leaving them to stare at each other in the growing darkness ...

Further up the long troop train, other members of the Regiment who had been out before were settling down for the night. Positioning in the Bull's wagon was based on rank. During daylight hours, he and his cronies, the Kitchen Bulls, squatted by the door so that they could see as much of the landscape flitting by as possible, and be first off when hot rations were served or a 'piss pause' was ordered. But at night the Bull and the Kitchen Bulls claimed the places nearest the stove as their right. Next came the old heads, Red Rudi, Deltgen and the rest of the old 69th. Then at the outer extremities of the freezingly cold car where the moisture on the wooden walls had already turned to ice, were the 'greenbeaks' as they were called, the youths who had never been out before and were getting their first introduction into the strange world of the Front.

Now as the crowded wagon started to thicken with blue cigarette smoke and the Bull relaxed by the glowing stove with a drink from one of the flatmen carried by his kitchen toadies, René Deltgen began to further the military education of the greenbeaks closest to him.

'Up there, there's creepers of all shapes and sizes. Mosquitoes that can blow up yer kisser to the size of a football in no time. But the lice are the worse, aren't they Rudi?' Deltgen's humorous, flat face beamed at them.

'If you say so,' his running-mate conceded gloomily, staring at the flickering shadows, distorted and magnified grotesquely by the flames.

'There's many a time I've counted up to a couple of hundred of 'em feeding on my alabaster torso — and the little sods feed *twelve times daily*, remember that! They lay five eggs a day and them eggs survive ten days on one meal of blood so...' he did a quick calculation while his horrified young listeners began to wriggle and scratch, as if they were already infected. 'So in two weeks, if you don't do a little bit of pest control, you could have a thousand of 'em nibbling at yer armpits and crotch. There's many a time I've pulled a couple of dozen of the little grey darlings out of me foreskin!' He grinned maliciously at his sickened listeners. 'Of course there's rats, too. Whoppers they are, cos of all the good German grub they've got to feed on. God, how them Ivan rats do like a good old German stubble-hopper's corpse!'

'Knock it off, you plush-arsed misery,' Red Rudi growled. 'You'll have 'em all creaming their skivvies even before they see the sodding Front.'

'Only trying to enlighten them, that's all, Rudi,' Deltgen replied cheerfully. 'Bit of practical training you might say. Like how to burn up lice eggs with a candle or take the ginger out of 'em when you've strafed 'em a bit with louse-powder. That is if those thieving quartermaster bulls haven't already flogged it to some base stallion.' He looked pointedly at the Bull, who was well known in the Regiment for his black market activities with any supplies he could get his big paws on.

The Bull concentrated on the flatman handed him by the sergeant cook, one of his special cronies. He knew better than to tangle with Deltgen and Red Rudi; they knew too much about him.

'Mind you,' Deltgen continued, 'the flies can be shitting awful, especially when you're near a cavalry division. Last time we went up we were with one. How those nags crap! One of their sergeants was telling me that six thousand nags in yer average cavalry division can produce forty tons of shit per day, and so you greenbeaks can imagine the flies you have around that stuff — some of 'em as big as a canary and a sting on 'em like the kick of a mule. I'm telling you lads, the Popovs are bad, but the crummy vermin's worse,' and with that Deltgen sighed and leaned back on his pack.

'Sermon over for the night, Father?' Red Rudi queried with a sneer on his ever-angry face and then to the recruits, 'All right, you greenbeaks, get yer heads down now. Where we're going, you'll be lucky if you can saw wood once a week. Good-night!'

Now the 'good-nights' started to come from all sides. At the stove, the Bull thrust home another log and settled down too with his back to the warmth. Here and there an old head began to snore, but there were many that night who couldn't sleep. Listening to the monotonous roll and beat of the troop-train's wheels, they were lost in dreams, their gaze trying to penetrate the red-glowing gloom, minds full of sombre shadows and dark forebodings. They were going 'up'. That they knew, but what lay ahead in the ghost-ridden wastes of that land which awaited them? What indeed?…

'*Polacks*,' someone exclaimed, as along the length of the long train the sliding doors were thrown open to let in the keen morning air, for waiting ragged women and children swarmed forward, hands held out as they begged for bread in German and Polish. Here and there a generous veteran threw out a crust, but they scarcely had enough for themselves. Besides this was the first stop since the previous night the overflowing latrine buckets compelled the men to swarm out of the cars and rush for the nearest embankment. Soon the whole length of the train was flanked by naked backsides and the begging Polish women scurried their children away from the sight of so much bare maleness.

'The New Order,' Colonel von Dietz commented cynically as he and the Pill strolled the length of the train smoking and enjoying the fresh air, 'the benefits of the One Thousand Year Reich bestowed on the grateful natives, eh, Pill?'

The doctor puffed on his pipe and watched a ragged child, stomach swollen with hunger, eyes bulging from an emaciated face, rummaging in the trash thrown out of the officers' wagon. 'A lot of people say they didn't have a pot to piss in before the war as it was, Horst,' he said.

'Now we've even taken the piss from them.'

'I suppose you're right, Horst,' the doctor conceded, routinely inspecting the men's faeces as he walked at von Dietz's side. He threw a side-glance at his companion's thin handsome face with the bitter, turned-down lips of a man who had been disappointed in life. 'But you know, you mustn't take all these things so seriously — that fellow shot yesterday at the station, these Poles, the things that are going to happen once we get to the Front. If you do, you'll crack under the strain.'

Von Dietz stopped and smiled down at him. 'Pill, you need not fear for my mental health. I am a born survivor. My principles went out of the window in 1939. The only thing that concerns me is the Regiment and the survival of the men. That's all. There'll be time for moralizing — and,' von Dietz instinctively lowered his voice, as did everyone in Germany these days in case the Gestapo was listening, '*perhaps decisive action at the top* after the war has ended.'

The Pill nodded his agreement and changed the subject hastily, for it was a dangerous one, even out here in remotest Poland. 'What about anti-partisan guards, Horst?'

'As soon as we reach Vinnitza immediately we cross into Russia, though I hardly think we'll encounter many partisans at the town which houses the Führer's own headquarters, do you...' Suddenly von Dietz stopped short.

'What is it?'

By way of answer, the tall young Colonel pointed up the track, where what looked like a great worm was crawling across the snow. Even at that distance the two officers could smell the biting stench it gave off and the subdued hum that came from it like that of a busy beehive. 'Prisoners,' he said, 'Russian prisoners.'

The men squatting along the track were rising now to their feet and pulling up their trousers to view the Russians. Even the Polish women and children forgot their hunger as the earth-brown skeletons lurched towards them, stumbling and staggering ever onwards, those that lagged behind cruelly lashed by the whips of the elderly guards on ponies.

Now they were almost on the spectators, giving off that filthy stench which reminded von Dietz of the monkey houses of the zoos of his youth. Their faces were like death, but some had eyes which burned with such hatred at the sight of the German soldiers that von Dietz feared for one fleeting moment that his body would be consumed by it.

'Holy strawsack!' Deltgen exclaimed, as one of the Russians, an emaciated giant with a blood-stained bandage dangling from his head, staggered from the ranks only to be set upon by one of the guards, who belaboured him with his whip until, the back of his tunic dripping with blood, the Russian begged for mercy. '*What swine!*'… '*Stop it, you bastards!*… *You ought to have a taste of that lash yersens!*' The cries of outrage and anger went up on all sides from the watching infantrymen, while one of the greenbeaks, shaken by the horror of the sight, started to sob softly.

But in the end the long column of prisoners had passed and at the end of the column the lone guard on horseback, whose job it obviously was to finish off stragglers, for he had a loaded pistol in his free hand, bent from his horse and said, half amused, half apologetic, 'What's all the fuss about, comrades? They're only Russkis you know, comrades — not human beings.'

Red Rudi's hand flashed down to his bayonet and there was naked menace in his burning gaze. 'Fuck off you!' he snarled, 'and quick, if you know what's good for you!… And don't you dare call us your comrades!'

The guard spurred his horse into a gallop and shot off, head hunched between bent shoulders, as if he half expected a slug in his back at any moment. A second later the NCOs were blowing their whistles and the locomotive let off a hiss of steam to indicate the driver was ready to move once more. The second stage of the long journey to the Front had commenced.

But the 69th Regiment was not fated to reach Vinnitza and the Russian border that day. Not long after the troop train had started to chug through the area leading up to the fortress of Przemysl, where there had been severe fighting back in 1941, the driver was signalled to take a switch-line. Urgent traffic was coming west from the Front.

'Casualties probably,' von Dietz commented as their train started to slow down and enter what was left of a small town, with its shattered, rusting Russian and German tanks lying here and there among the ruins.

'I should expect so,' the Pill agreed, taking his eyes off piles of ruins, with the houses cut in two, revealing the domestic intimacies of their interiors. 'Good thing too. Never does for troops to see casualties when they're going up. It's unsettling...' He stopped short and craned forward, trying to make out the heavy-set figure standing on the platform in front of them.

'What is it?' von Dietz asked as the locomotive's wheels clattered noisily and the train began to slow down.

'I do believe that it's old Santa Claus himself standing out there!'

Von Dietz's face brightened. 'You mean *that* Santa Claus?' he exclaimed.

'I certainly do.'

'Well, then the boys *will* be happy.' Von Dietz rose to his feet hurriedly and started to buckle on his helmet and pistol. 'This will be a little bonus for them... Perhaps it'll take their minds off what's to come, Pill.'

The Pill rubbed his hands professionally. 'There'll be work for old Pill this day, I'll be bound.'

Squatting in the straw at the far end of the wagon, shivering a little as the cold air streamed in from the open door, Ensign von Doerr asked puzzled, 'But who is Santa Claus, sir? And what does he do?'

Von Dietz grinned down at him, as he adjusted his helmet. 'Santa Claus, von Doerr, is one of the most important men on the Eastern Front. Better than a whole week of Request Concerts and Front Theatres put together. He runs Mobile

Brothel Number Ten. It's famous throughout the Front. Come on, Pill, let's go and see what he's to offer the men.'

'Well, Santa Claus, how are things?' von Dietz asked, as he faced the crimson-faced sergeant with his shock of white hair and heavy paunch. 'Oh, for God's sake, don't play soldier, stand at ease!'

With a sigh of relief the fat brothel-keeper relaxed and returned von Dietz's smile. Behind him in the house which now functioned as Mobile Brothel Number Ten, the 'girls' hung out of the windows in spite of the cold, and somewhere someone was playing a piano rather well. 'Not so bad, sir. Not so bad.'

'Any new meat since the last time you serviced the 69th — and no jokes please, Santa Claus,' the Pill said, holding up his hand, as if to ward off any attempt at humour.

''Fraid not, Doctor,' the big NCO said, his voice rumbling from somewhere down in his ample stomach. 'You can imagine that we don't exactly get the cream out here. But they're good whores as whores go. Serviced a whole regiment of Italians going up last week. Polished off the whole lot of 'em in two hours — and you know what gluttons for sex those men are!'

Von Dietz smiled at Santa Claus's choice of words and said, 'Listen, it seems we're going to be held up here for a while. Can you see the Regiment gets through on time?'

'Of course, sir.' Santa Claus looked from left to right to check if he were being overheard. 'But I don't think you'll be in that much of a hurry.'

'What do you mean, you old rogue?'

'There's been a lot of movement east these last ten days. Plenty of supply trains following up too. Bit strange for this time of the year, sir, ain't it?' He tugged down the edge of his right eyelid. 'Wooden eye, be on your guard,' he used the serviceman's phrase.

'And what's that supposed to mean?' Dietz asked, as the Pill turned to carry out his medical duties now that the brothel was open to them...

'Can't be specific, sir, but there's something in the wind — a new offensive perhaps. Who knows? Now if you'll excuse me, sir, I'll ready my ladies to do their bit for Folk, Fatherland and Führer,' and with a solemn wink he left von Dietz to his own thoughts.

'All right then last batch — *lift the curtain*!'

At the Pill's command, the last group of men for the brothel, standing in the snow, shivering with their trousers and underpants around their ankles absurdly lifted the flaps of their grey issue shirts.

As quickly as he could, the Pill walked along their ranks, glancing at their genitals, stopping occasionally when he was not altogether satisfied to examine the organs in more detail, while behind him the preceding batch were washing out the same organs with a solution of potassium permanganate carried in long rubber tubes from the purple-coloured bottles above their heads, whistling happily as they did so.

Satisfied finally, the Pill turned to a waiting and beaming Santa Claus, 'All right, Father Christmas, they're all certified clean and fit for human consumption. They're yours now.'

'Thank you, sir,' Santa Claus touched his gloved hand to his greasy cap in a sloppy salute. 'All of you, listen to me,' he cried above the hiss of escaping steam from the locomotive. 'No pushing, no shoving. Everybody'll get a go. *One go only* — and use a Parisian . No Parisian, no jig-a-jig, got it?'

'Hurry it up, Sarge,' Red Rudi called, tugging at his pants, his cheeks red with cold. 'If we don't get inside soon, my outside-plumbing'll be froze up!'

'Don't worry, laddie,' Santa Claus replied in high good humour. 'My girls could make a mummy perform. All right, that's it. Have yer money and yer log of wood at the ready. At the count of three start to move forward. *One ... two ... three...*'

Von Dietz shook his head as he watched his men shuffle forward in the snow, money in one hand, log of wood for heating the whore house in the other. In this fourth year of war, even sex had become regimented, carried out by numbers, he told himself. Then he forgot Santa Claus and his brothel. Poor as the facilities were, the men were overjoyed at the chance of love-making one last time before they went up. He sat down in the little room which Santa Claus had offered him until the line east was cleared and they could start moving again.

Outside in the kitchen, the big Polish woman who was Santa Claus's mistress was frying potatoes and eggs on the stove, her cheeks aflame with the heat, as the eggs spluttered and the potatoes seethed in the fat; all around her soldiers who, still had money to pay for the food squeezed together drinking weak beer and ersatz coffee, their collars open at the neck, sweat glistening in their eyebrows like opaque pearls. To von Dietz they all looked so alive and happy. It seemed hardly believable that soon a tremendous change would take place in those boys, who sat there laughing and joking and making ribald remarks at the big Polish woman — those who would survive.

Von Dietz lay back on the sofa, feet up, hands behind his head, watching the shadows of the night beginning to creep in through the little steamed-up window. Already the sickle moon had begun to rise to mellow the grey afternoon sky. Soon they would have to put up the blackout.

The talk, the chatter, the sound of spluttering fat receded into the distance. From far, far away came the mournful whistle of some long train on the main line. Save for that there was nothing but the spectral whisper of the night breeze in the skeletal trees outside. Suddenly von Dietz was overcome by a great sadness, he did not know why. Was it the faces of those happy boys in the kitchen? The eerie quality of the dying day? Or was it the knowledge that on the morrow they would be there — at the Front?

Slowly the tall lean man, stretched out on the sofa, drifted off into sleep, his body perfectly still, his chest hardly rising. A casual observer entering the room at that moment might well have thought he was dead...

CHAPTER 3

'Would you follow me, gentlemen?' the guide said, as if he were some kind of domestic servant rather than an NCO in a regular infantry battalion. 'The going is a bit tricky and we don't like to attract any attention.'

'Friend Ivan?' von Dietz queried. Behind him the men were now forming up into combat march groups, on both sides of the snowbound road, a road pressed iron-hard by the wheels of countless vehicles and stained yellow with the urine of the thousands of horses that had passed this way up to the Front.

'Yes, sir,' said the NCO, a big West Prussian, warmly clothed in a goatskin with what looked like a woman's fur tippet tightly wrapped around his neck. 'They've got observation posts over there,' he indicated with a gloved hand the faint blur on the hard-blue winter horizon which was the besieged city of Leningrad, 'and we can always expect them to catch us with our knickers down with one of those sewing machines of theirs.' He tugged the end of his long, dripping nose. 'And they've still got plenty of artillery and ammo. They'd make a nasty mess of us if they caught us on the open road.'

As the CO gave the signal for the regiment to advance, Ensign von Doerr, who had overheard the conversation saw the strange pink silent flickering on the blue horizon. 'What's that, soldier?' he asked curiously, as they moved off.

'Nothing much, sir,' Red Rudi answered, not attempting to conceal his contempt at the officer's lack of knowledge, 'just the permanent barrage.'

'Barrage! But I can't hear anything.'

'Don't worry, sir,' Rudi replied, 'you will soon enough, once the shot and shit starts dropping in our direction.'

'Oh my God!' von Doerr gulped, his boyish face suddenly very white.

'Oh my God indeed,' Rudi chuckled at the officer's obvious fear. Then he, like the rest of the veterans, concentrated on getting into the trench line as quickly as possible before the Popovs spotted them.

Now there was a heavy brooding silence about the snowbound countryside. They filed past gunners dug in in the fields on both sides of the country road, but they did not seem to see the newcomers and went about their duties solemnly, their faces serious and thoughtful like men attending a funeral. They came across a group of ambulance drivers and stretcher-bearers smoking in silence, clustered around a fire, occasionally warming their hands with slow, deliberate movements, their eyes sad as they saw the heavily-laden infantry approach. It was the same as they marched by a group of cooks stoking up the goulash-cannon cooking the rations for the evening meal. Instead of being sad, they looked shamed, as if they felt themselves somehow inferior to these newcomers, safe and warm in their humble tasks.

'Is it always like this, soldier?' von Doerr asked, recovered now a little from his initial shock. 'So ... so empty really, apart from the odd individual like those handful of cooks back there.'

Red Rudi shrugged carelessly and remained silent, too contemptuous to bother to answer the officer's stupid question, but Deltgen took pity on von Doerr. 'It's always like this, sir,' he explained, 'the closer you get to the Front, the emptier it gets. You see they only put idiots in the infantry. The smart fellers — they get into the quartermaster branch, the service corps and the like. The battlefield they leave to us — the poor bleeding stubble-hoppers, see?'

Von Doerr swallowed hard, 'I see,' he said in a strangled voice. Suddenly he understood what those two hundred years of family tradition which had led him into volunteering for the Regiment at the age of 17 had meant — all those yellowing portraits on the family walls, the dusty banners, the battered military trophies. It meant this war-torn forlorn countryside over which they now trailed like homeless insignificant ants.

They started to file through a patch of shell-shattered woodland, the trees stark black and skeletal, with their branches ripped off and hanging like severed limbs. To their right was a charred, burnt-out isba . Next to it three naked bodies were hanging from the trees, frozen to stone, the rope buried deep in abnormally long necks, the tongues hanging out like dried blackened leather. One was a heavily bosomed woman, her bare breasts hanging down almost to her waist, and, attached to each nipple, a small cowbell of the type the Russian peasants hung around the necks of their animals to prevent them wandering.

'Partisans,' the guide said laconically.

Von Dietz rubbed the back of his gloved hand across his cracked lips and stared at the woman's bluish feet, the soles black with filth. 'Why the bells?' he asked.

The guide shrugged. 'The stubble-hoppers' idea of a joke, sir. You know what they're like up here?'

As the horrified greenbeaks started to move past, a faint wind caught the clappers of the bells and they began to toll…

The men filing out to meet them were silent and hard eyed, bodies clad in anything warm so that they looked more like a crowd of motley civilians than soldiers. There was something insolent in the way they tightened their belts and hawked to spit into the snow, as if they were contemptuous of the newcomers, even resentful that they should look so clean and healthy, while they were dirty, unshaven, undernourished, their eyes bulging and gleaming out of their skull-like faces.

Ensign von Doerr exchanged salutes with the lieutenant whose sector he was going to take over.

The officer, an undersized, skinny-chested, bespectacled fellow who looked more like a school teacher than a soldier, although his chest was covered with decorations, looked von Doerr up and down until the latter blushed. Then he said, 'Well, young hero, after tin , eh?'

The Ensign's blush deepened. 'Well, no ... not really, sir,' he stuttered.

'Well you'll get it here — if you live.' Suddenly the Lieutenant's red-rimmed eyes blazed furiously behind his nickel-rimmed spectacles and he made a clutching gesture at his skinny chest, as if he were about to rip his decorations off and give them to an astonished von Doerr. 'You can have 'em off me, you know, you fucking idealist...! You don't have to get yerself shot for Folk, Fatherland and Führer for a bit of enamel and a pretty black and white ribbon! You can —' He stopped as abruptly as he had started and for one instant von Doerr thought he was going to break down and sob. But he caught himself in time. 'Sorry,' he said and turned away, leaving von Doerr to stare in amazement at his skinny shoulders.

'They're all *meschugge*, Ensign,' Deltgen tried to reassure the astonished young officer. 'They always are when they come out of the line. We'll be the same, I don't doubt, when we come out. You see the old heads resent us, even if we've got a chestful of tin ourselves. They think we've been having a right old high time back in the Homeland — wine, women and song

— while they've been sitting out the shite up here.' He tweaked the end of his red dripping nose with his two fingers and expertly flung the snot away before it dripped on his tunic. 'Don't pay any heed to them. When you've been up the line long enough, you always get to be half nuts.' He tapped his forehead significantly and pressed himself back against an earthwork, as yet another batch of these strange, bearded, ragged veterans, all of them wild-eyed and muttering to themselves, came lurching out of their positions. 'Couldn't let that lot loose in civvy street now,' he commented when they had gone, 'they'd tear the shitting place apart! *All meschugge!*'

Von Doerr stared at their front, as the first flare sailed into the air from the Russian positions and hung there for a while so that the whole countryside shimmered with a dazzlingly bright white light before it sank again, to leave no-man's land flooded with a curious eerie luminosity. He shivered violently. The uncertain shadows out there suggested a world of ghosts…

'So far it's been a real old Ghost Front,' the CO of the departing regiment explained. A gaunt giant in a dirty sheepskin with an ordinary infantryman's rifle slung over his shoulder, his stained uniform bore no badges of rank — snipers, von Dietz told himself automatically — and on his feet the CO wore clumsy looted Russian felt *valinka*, one of them split at the toe, as if he might be suffering from frostbite.

The two Colonels stood in the shelter of the breastworks beyond where the soldiers were exchanging positions, von Dietz listening with professional curiosity to the other man whose regiment had been in the line in front of the besieged city for nearly a month now.

'How long?' he asked finally, after absorbing Colonel Moeller's statement about it being a quiet front.

'About three kilometres. That should give you a kilometre per battalion so if you're up to strength...'

Von Dietz nodded that he was.

'You'll have about one man to every two metres, that is if you're content only to man the front line.'

Von Dietz stared at the intricate trench lines which had grown up around Leningrad in the year and a half that it had been besieged by the Wehrmacht. They were made up of three parallel lines — the fire-trench, support-trench, and connecting travel-trenches. All three were constructed in a dog-tooth arrangement with bays at every ten metres or so, so that bomb and shell blast were minimized and the men behind the parapets could not be enfiladed from the flanks if the enemy somehow managed to seize one end of the trench. Most of the trenches were about a metre and a half deep, in spite of the frozen, iron-hard earth of the area, with another metre of sandbags on top so that in the fire-trench at least a man could stand upright. In the others he would have to move bent double if he didn't want to get shot by a sniper. The other two systems were more complicated, for they housed kitchens, latrines, storehouses, first-aid posts, all blown three metres deep into the permafrost by explosives. All in all it was a formidable position — *for defensive purposes.*

'Losses?' he queried finally.

'Ten per cent,' Colonel Moeller answered. 'Frostbite, snipers, artillery in that order — and self-inflicted wounds.' He frowned. 'At least two a day.'

Von Dietz said nothing. Moeller's infantry were regular, but they weren't the 69th with its tradition. In his Regiment there would be no self-inflicted wounds.

Moeller seemed to be able to read the other man's mind. 'Morale is good, don't misunderstand me, von Dietz. The men are loyal, brave and obedient. But there is something about this Front,' he shivered. 'It gets to them. The tricks they've learnt in order to get away with self-inflicted wounds. We caught a sergeant last week who had shot his big toe off through a moistened loaf of bread to avoid showing powder burns ...'

'You said, "something about this Front",' von Dietz interrupted the other Colonel, his face curious.

Colonel Moeller looked at him. 'Did I? All right, von Dietz, I'll give it to you straight. It's this northern light, it's the thought that over there in Leningrad there are thousands — hundreds of thousands — of people starving, living like dogs, it's the kind of heavy brooding silence that comes over the place.' He screwed up his brow angrily. 'Oh, I don't know. I haven't got a gift with words. I'm just a damned hair-arsed stubble-hopper like my men — no poet. All I know is the place gets to me and my men. I'll be glad to go and I'll tell you straight that if I go back next time and we're up to a hot front, I won't object. Nor, I think, will my boys. I've had enough of the Ghost Front.' He stuck out his big hand and von Dietz noted that the nails had been bitten down to the quick, as if Moeller had chewed them a lot in his nervousness. 'Best of luck, Colonel and your 69th.'

'Thanks. You as well, Colonel.'

Half an hour later the veterans had gone and the men shivering in the night wind, lining the parapets of the fire-trench for the first time, realized that they were alone. They were up front, in the line at last. Slowly the winter night began to fall...

CHAPTER 4

The night was very dark. A freezing wind swept across the snow waste to their front, chilling the men huddled in the fire-trench to the bone. Men crouched with their collars drawn up high over their ears, breathing hard into the rough fabric so that their warm breath might heat the frozen tips of their dripping noses a little, silent and apprehensive.

To their front all was silent. There was no movement, no activity save the white flares hushing noiselessly into the sky above Leningrad to explode in a burst of brilliant white stars. Then they sank to the earth again like fallen angels, hovering for an instant at dead point before extinguishing, leaving the watching men's imaginations racing, the uncertain shadows suggesting a world of ghosts.

Ensign von Doerr, on watch, paced the trench anxiously, his mind racing, seeing things stir everywhere, terrifying Russian giants about to leap upon him turned out to be no more than a snow-heavy bush or some shattered, rusting remnant of old battles. Time and time again he tried to reason with himself, telling his racing brain that the nearest Russians were half a kilometre away, that no one in his right mind, even a Russian, would venture out on a freezing cold night like this, with the mercury already well below twenty degrees. But his brain refused to obey him and he felt as if he were experiencing some frightening nightmare which at any moment could explode into terrifying, violent action.

Another hour passed. Von Dietz, huddled in a fur-collared greatcoat without badges, an ordinary infantryman's rifle slung over his shoulder, passed down the freezing line, whispering encouragement to the weary soldiers guarding it, patting a shoulder here, making a soft joke there, momentarily taking away the terror from the night.

'All well?' he asked von Doerr.

'Yes, sir. Thank you, sir,' the youngster forced himself to answer through teeth which chattered, not only with the cold.

To their front another white flare hissed into the air and for a few moments von Dietz caught sight of the other man's frightened face in the intense white light. He placed his hand on his arm reassuringly. 'Don't worry, boy,' he said gently. 'It happens to us all — the first time. None of us are heroes you know … just actors once we're in command. We have to be to impress the men. Remember that, lad — not heroes but simply actors. Good-night.' And with that, he passed on, back to his dugout in the supply-trench.

For a few moments von Doerr was reassured, telling himself that the CO, in spite of his harsh face and bitter drooping mouth, was a good fellow who understood what went on in a man's mind, although his own features rarely revealed any emotion. For a moment or two he wondered what had gone wrong with von Dietz's own life to make him look like that — cold, reserved, unyielding. Was it the loneliness of command? The great responsibility he had to bear for the lives of some three thousand men? Or was it something else, something more personal?

Then his own fear overcame him again and he forgot the CO and his comforting words. He saw a shadow move. It was a man, he knew it was! He froze. I won't stir a finger, he told himself, his mind racing furiously. It's not looking for me anyway — it *can't* be! 'Oh, dear God,' he prayed with sudden fervent fury, 'don't let it…' he broke off abruptly. A faint breeze had agitated the shadow and he could hear the slither of falling snow. It was a bush! With a hand that shook violently, Ensign von Doerr wiped the hot sweat of fear from his brow, and began to walk down the fire-trench once more, his legs feeling like rubber.

'*Women*!' Deltgen pontificated. 'That's the only thing that makes life worth living for your ordinary feller. Juicy women… If them at the top didn't promise a bit of sex every now and again, do you think they'd ever be able to force us to do this lark?'

Red Rudi grunted and one of the greenbeaks said, 'But Senior Soldier, they'd shoot yer with a firing squad if yer didn't do what they ordered.'

Deltgen smiled appeased. 'I'm glad that some of your young wet-tails have a bit o' respect for rank,' he said to a gloomy Rudi, who in the glowing light of another flare was peering over the parapet into the shimmering no-man's land. '*Senior Soldier*, that's it, lad! Keep it up and I'll put a good word in for you with the CO. But all the same,' Deltgen continued, returning to his subject, 'that's the only way they can tame us — *sex*! If there weren't the promise of that, you might as well be shittingly well dead anyhow. Remember the case…'

'Trap!' Rudi cut into this new anecdote fiercely.

Deltgen's hands tensed on his rifle. Around him the greenbeaks froze, fear suddenly written across their ashen young faces. 'What is it, Rudi?'

'There's somebody out there,' Rudi whispered through gritted teeth, not turning his head away from the front.

'Come off it, you're seeing things,' Deltgen retorted, yet suddenly his voice was cast in a hushed whisper too.

'Have a look…'

The sudden single shot drowned the rest of Rudi's angry words.

'*Mother!*' one of the greenbeaks gasped with fear as Deltgen flung himself against the parapet, rifle up and aimed in one and the same gesture.

Together the two running-mates scanned their front. The man that Rudi had spotted had vanished, but now Deltgen knew that his friend had not been mistaken. He couldn't see the Russians, but he could smell them all right. There was no mistaking that distinctive odour of theirs, composed of the sour smell of vodka, human sweat and the coarse black *marhoka* tobacco they smoked. The Popovs were out there in the snowy, shell-holed waste somewhere!

'Stand to, you shits!' he hissed. 'At the double now — and for Chrissake, don't fire and give our positions away until you have to!'

Excited and fearful, the greenbeaks flung themselves against the sandbags, lifting their weapons, their eyes, wide and staring, their breath suddenly harsh and shallow and loud.

The minutes passed. Rudi and Deltgen relaxed a little, as they swung their gazes from left to right, keeping them low in the fashion of old soldiers so that they could see anything silhouetted a darker black against the horizon. Now Red Rudi was beginning to believe that he had been wrong after all; that his eyes had perhaps played tricks. It was their first time in the line for a long time.

'*Look!*' Deltgen said urgently at his side. '*Ten o'clock!*'

Tall dark figures were beginning to dart through the shattered skeletal trees to their left. Bending almost double, they would rush forward a couple of metres, throw themselves to the ground, wait and then jump up again. Deltgen swallowed hard. Even to a battle-hardened veteran like himself, there was something ghost-like and eerie about this silent approach. 'Hold yer fire,' he hissed, not recognizing his own voice. 'I'll have the eggs off anybody who fires before I give the word — *with a blunt razor-blade*!'

Thus they waited as the ghostly figures got closer and closer, feeling their way obviously, as if they did not quite know where the German positions were. Two hundred metres ... one hundred and fifty ... one hundred...

Deltgen looked at Rudi enquiringly.

The latter nodded and said, 'I think they've come far enough.'

'They're only probing, yer know, Rudi. It's S.O.P. when new troops come in the line opposite them. Oughtn't to do anything without an officer's permission.'

'Well, where *is* the wet-arsed shit?' Rudi countered gruffly, as the tall dark figures came ever closer. 'Does he want a shitting written invite?' He bent his head over his rifle and tucked the stock well into his right shoulder. 'It's now or never!' Next instant he pressed his trigger. A Russian screamed and flailed the air momentarily with his outstretched arms before he flopped to the ground.

That single shot broke the last of Ensign von Doerr's courage. As firing erupted all along the German line and a great hoarse angry 'urrah' came from the Russians, the young officer sank huddled into the cover of a bomb-bay, his trousers wet with his own urine, hands tightly held across his eyes like a child trying to blot out a nightmare and began to sob...

'*URRAH*! ... *URRAH* ... *URRAH*!' the yell came from a hundred or more throats, as the Russians surged forward in a ragged line, tommy guns chattering at their hips as they ran. Now the greenbeaks propped up against the sandbags forgot their fear, carried away by the heady excitement of sudden battle, overcome by that primeval unreasoning blood-lust which transforms all men, brave and cowardly, once they are committed to combat and there is no other escape. Now it had become a matter of kill or be killed.

Still the Russians came, men falling all the time, but their comrades springing over the writhing figures on the ground, determined to penetrate the German line. Up on the parapet Rudi and Deltgen fired, ejected the cartridge case, aimed and fired again, carrying out the movements with mechanical expertise, as if they were back on some peacetime range, hardly aware that each shot they fired killed or maimed a man, mindless to the screams, the cries of rage, the rattle of machine-gun fire and the pounding of Russian boots as they rushed ever closer.

And then suddenly, the Russian who had been intoning the 'urrah' in a high tenor voice to be responded to by the others in a hoarse roar had ceased, and the survivors of that first wave were springing into the fire-trench, concentrating now on the bloody work ahead, no breath left for cheering any longer.

Von Doerr screamed with horror, as a burly figure sprang clear over the sandbags and dropped on his feet in a cat-like crouch in front of him. '*No!*' he screamed in an ecstasy of terror, as the Russian raised his round-barrelled tommy gun, an evil smile of triumph on his yellow, pockmarked face. '*NO … PLEASE…*' He threw up his hands, as if naked flesh might ward off the steel bullets. '*NO!*'

A knife of scarlet flame stabbed the gloom to the rear. The Russian screamed pitifully and stumbled forward, carrying von Doerr with him, his blood jetting out and drenching the young officer's horrified face. Feet pounded over his back, as he lay trapped by the dying Russian. Screams, curses, yells, cries of agony — they filled the air on all sides. He could hear men gasping harshly as if in the last throes of sexual excitement. Men called out in a language he could not understand. At his side the Russian's spine contorted in absolute agony. His fingers sought and found von Doerr's arm. They dug deep in the flesh holding him in a cruel vice-like grip, digging and digging, as if they were trying to hold on to life itself. And then with a soft moan the Russian fell back, dead.

His death seemed to act as a signal for the others. Throwing away their weapons they clawed and fought their way up the sandbags, the Germans stabbing at their backs with their gleaming red bayonets, yelling obscenities, terrible sexual obscenities, as they thrust their blades pleasurably into the soft yielding flesh of the enemy shoulders, withdrawing them with a wet sucking sound. And then it was over, and there was no sound save that of the moans of the wounded and the soft sobbing of one of the greenbeaks, crying like a little child with a broken heart.

It was thus that von Dietz and the Pill found the Ensign, surrounded by the Soviet dead, still lying there in the dirty snow, stained pink by the blood of the dying, crawling futilely in their stubborn attempts to escape their fate.

'Von Doerr,' the Pill called, 'are you hurt?'

There was no reply. The Pill bent over him, while von Dietz turned to Deltgen and Rudi who were bending over the Soviet dead going from one man to the next, rifles still held at the ready. 'What happened, Deltgen?' he demanded.

'The usual, sir, for the first night in the line. They were sounding us out.' He pulled up a Russian by his shaggy hair and then let the head fall again with a soft thud; the man had been hit in the face. He was dead all right. Where his nose had once been there was now a gaping scarlet hole.

Von Dietz nodded his understanding. 'Good work, the two of you. Now back to your posts. I'll send up Sergeant-Major Bulle with a relief party straight away. They can take over and clear up this mess. It'll be a matter of minutes now.'

'Will they come again, sir?' one of the greenbeaks asked out of the crimson-glowing darkness, for over the Soviet lines red alarm rockets were shooting into the night sky everywhere, to signal the attack had failed and the survivors were coming back through their own positions.

'Friend Ivan?... Oh, yes, he'll be back all right. He's a very persistent chap, old Friend Ivan is — and he doesn't particularly like us being here, you know.'

The men chuckled, even the greenbeaks, and then they started to trail back, their shoulders bowed, as if with sudden exhaustion. The Pill remained, he was watching von Doerr who had staggered to his feet and was leaning against the side of the parapet, then he turned to von Dietz, a querying look on his wise old face.

Von Dietz shrugged and said, 'Give him a shot of vodka, a tablet to make him sleep and we'll see from there.'

As if the hangdog young Ensign was not even there, the Pill said, 'But that won't solve the problem, Horst, you know.'

'It's the only solution I can think of now,' von Dietz replied. 'And if that doesn't do the trick, the Russians or —' he hesitated for barely a fraction of a second, 'a firing squad will do it for us. Now see that he is sedated, Pill.' And with that he turned and hurried off to call out Bulle and the relief party, the problem of Ensign von Doerr's cowardice forgotten for the time being.

CHAPTER 5

By the third day of their sojourn up-front, most of the soldiers of the 69th Regiment were lousy and not a few of the officers too. It was common enough on the Eastern Front and most of the old heads had long got used to the fact, though the greenbeaks almost always reacted with horror on first finding the fat little creatures and their eggs lining their clothing. Indeed one of them, encouraged by an amused Deltgen and Red Rudi, took his shirt to Bulle and asked formally, if he couldn't have another one, because 'this one has certain insects in it, Sarnt-Major.'

'What did you say?' Bulle said, his beefy face turning crimson, his suspicious little red piglike eyes turning in the direction of Deltgen and Red Rudi, both of whom were attempting to appear as innocent bystanders. 'Certain insects? What kind of insects?'

The innocent had held up his infested shirt. 'I think they call them — lice, Sarnt-Major,' he had answered earnestly. 'And I've read that the Führer insists his soldiers should be as speedy as a greyhound, hard as Krupp steel, tough as leather — and perfectly cl...' His voice trailed away into nothing, as the purple veins began to tick alarmingly at the side of the Bull's crimson face.

'You arse with ears — make legs before I feed you, hair and skin, the lot of your stupid frame to the ... *the insects!*' he had bellowed at the top of his voice, almost blowing away the innocent.

But in the end the problem had become too great and von Dietz had ordered that a determined effort should be made to eradicate the lice before the men started to report sick with the sores caused by scratching. The Pill supported him. On the black market of the rear echelon, cans of stolen *Wehrmacht* petrol were bought with the roubles they obtained from selling their own rations — illegally — to the surviving Russians of the area, and under the Pill's supervision a massive cleansing campaign was launched.

Thus once a day, every off-duty man was able to douse the seams of his lice-infested underclothing in petrol and although sickened by the stink of the gasoline was at least able to grab a few hours of untroubled sleep before going out into the freezing ominous night to do his spell on guard in the fire-trench.

For all of them, greenbeaks and old heads alike, night meant silence, isolation and unreasoning fear, time creeping by in the dark trench on leaden feet, as if it had almost stopped, the heavy brooding silence broken only by the occasional flare and the sudden heart-stopping rattle of a Soviet machine-gun.

In the darkness, even the most veteran men of the 69th became prey to all kinds of ridiculous fancies. A shattered tree stump took on a new and menacing form. A roll of rusting barbed wire would appear to move, be creeping forward frighteningly. A night noise would seem to be the hushed order of an advancing Russian patrol out to grab prisoners.

Then there was the ever-present danger of falling asleep, for by now all of them were virtually exhausted most of the time; the lice, the freezing cold, the bumpy discomfort of the dugout floors making sleep difficult even when they were off duty. Friends made agreements to keep each other awake over the hours, knowing that if they were caught asleep on duty, they could be punished by death; and at regular intervals they would whisper a few words to one another until that blissful moment when the relieving sentry would rap the soles of their boots, as they crouched above him on the parapet, to tell them that their spell of night duty was over at last.

So the 69th settled down to this new life in the trenches, happy to see each new day, glad of the invariable routine — the rifle-cleaning, the filling of sandbags, the repairing of the wire, the quick hand of *skat* — and dreading the night, even though it began with the high spot of the day: hot rations carried forward by fatigue parties in great clumsy hay-boxes.

That was until the sixth day when a new danger entered their lives...

It was a freezingly cold day. The frost had enfolded the war-torn front like a black cloak. In the fire-trench the sentries huddled deep in the collars of their greatcoats, their ears protected from frostbite by black ear-flaps, piles of straw heaped around their feet, their rifles coated with gleaming hoar-frost, their breath as dense as cigar smoke. Occasionally when the Soviets fired a shell at the German positions, it detonated with a hard metallic resonance on the iron-hard earth and what clods of soil it disturbed, were thrown high like lumps of granite.

It was midday when von Dietz, the Pill and the duty officer, Captain Heinze, a cocky Berliner who wore a black patch over the empty socket of his left eye, set off on their rounds along the fire-trench, trying to hide their own shivering from the miserable sentries who longed vainly to be relieved to the warmth of the dugouts.

'Great God!' Heinze exclaimed in his high-pitched Berlin accent, 'I do swear that it's colder than back in forty-one and I lost two toes and the back of my right heel that winter.' He grinned at the Pill, who he knew had strenuously objected to his returning to the Front with his one eye, saying, 'I know, Pill, I know. You're going to say in a minute there won't be much left of me if I go on like this.' He tapped his wadded jacket, below which rested his bemedalled tunic. 'I'm working my way to the Silver — then I'll retire and become a rear-echelon stallion, build up my gut and fornicate with all those plump office pigeons back at HQ.'

'You a rear-echelon stallion!' the Pill said sourly. 'I doubt for one instant that you mean it. Even if you did, your outside plumbing'll probably have frozen up permanently by that time.'

'Oh dear, don't you think I'd make a lovely soprano?' Heinze gushed in a shrill falsetto.

'Oh shut up, you two,' von Dietz said good humouredly, 'or the chaps will think you've got a little warm-brother love-nest going on in that dugout of yours.' Then he was businesslike again, as he paused in a bomb-bay packed high with crates of grenades and rifle ammunition. 'What's the situation to our front? Anything changed since dawn?' Heinze shook his head and then said, 'Well, nothing particular. Apart from a couple of what looked like drainage pipes which turned up after the last mortar stonk.' Von Dietz shot him a hard look. 'What was that?' he demanded, immediately suspicious.

Heinze's grin vanished. 'Do you think —'

'Well, it's the kind of trick Friend Ivan often pulls, isn't it?'

'Of course,' Heinze beat his gloved fist against the side of his helmet, 'it would be just like them to make us keep our turnips down with a few rounds of mortar fire while they sneak out and make a nice little nest for one of their rotten snipers in the piping.'

'Exactly. You know how Friend Ivan works. He puts a good man armed with a telescopic rifle inside a pipe and as soon as some fool sentry pops up his turnip, he has it promptly shot off by Friend Ivan — and nothing short of a direct hit can knock him out.'

The Pill looked at the two serious-faced officers as they stood, their breath wreathing their features in a thick grey. 'What's the drill?' he asked.

'Well, the first thing is to ensure that the sentries are on their guard one hundred per cent though in this deathly cold that is hard to do. Their movements are so damned sluggish. Then once he's given us a clue — that is the sniper — to where he is, we'll have to winkle him out.'

'The pipes?' Pill queried.

Von Dietz frowned. 'Well, on the face of it, that seems to be his nest. But it does appear a bit too obvious for Friend Ivan — he's damnably devious in these things.'

Heinze's grin returned. 'Well, there's one good way to find out, sir, isn't there?' he said heartily.

Von Dietz nodded. 'All right, are you on?'

'Of course.'

'Good.' Von Dietz bent and with his gloved hands scooped up an armful of the snow at his feet. Carefully he packed it on the top of his helmet, while the Pill stared at him in bewilderment.

Meanwhile Heinze walked to the end of the bomb-bay and picked up an entrenching tool which lay there. 'I'm ready, if you are,' he said.

Von Dietz nodded. 'All right, this is the way we'll work it,' he said. 'We'll triangulate by using my helmet to draw fire. We don't want to make it too obvious. Then if there is a Popov sniper out there, he *won't* be drawn by the usual helmet dodge. Hence the snow, making him think there is a carefully camouflaged spotter looking over the trench. As soon as he fires, Heinze note his position and —'

'Duck like hell!' Heinze beat him to it with a grin on his pink frozen face. 'All right, let's get on with it. I'm beginning to freeze to the floor.'

Hurriedly von Dietz seized the spade from the other officer and went to the right end of the bomb-bay. Heinze went to the opposite end.

'*Klar*?' von Dietz asked.

'*Klar*!'

Carefully avoiding dislodging the snow, von Dietz started to raise his helmet on the top of the entrenching tool, while the Pill's eyes flashed from one to the other of the two officers, tense with expectation.

'*Now*!' von Dietz rapped and raised it above the level of the trench, while in the same instant, Heinze brought his head cautiously above the sandbags.

There was the sharp dry crack of a high-velocity rifle-fire like the sound made by a twig being broken underfoot in a hot, summer wood. Heinze screamed shrilly and was thrown back from his position on the fire-step, as if he had been punched by some gigantic fist. He slammed against the opposite wall and slowly began to trail down it, the life ebbing out of him, dying as he fell, his other eye now gone, a scarlet suppurating pit where the steel bullet had ripped out the eye.

The Pill sprang to his aid. But it was already too late. As he raised Heinze, trying not to look at that terribly mutilated face, the bloody gore trickling down his pinched ashen cheek like squashed fig pulp, the dying man gulped ... 'Got silver ... now...' Next moment his head fell to one side and he was dead.

'*Curse God in Heaven*!' von Dietz roared, '*the Popov swine has tricked us...*'

Now a reign of terror commenced in the 69th's lines as the Russian snipers (for von Dietz reasoned that there were a number of them, and all of them experts) took their daily toll of those on duty in the fire-trench. The least slip and the sentry would be reeling gurgling and choking in his own blood with a bullet through his lungs, or dead without a sound, with a neat scarlet hole drilled in the centre of his forehead. Even the issue steel helmet didn't help, for at the close range the unknown killers operated from the high quality ammunition they used would penetrate the helmet, ripping the unfortunate sentry's skull apart with the fragments of flying steel.

Now the men were glad to be placed on sentry duty at night when the snipers did not operate. In some cases the men were so scared they had to be driven into the line during daylight hours, and only the constant presence of their officers in the fire-trench prevented them from burying even deeper into the earth and hiding themselves there till darkness fell.

Von Dietz spent the next seventy-two hours on constant duty in the fire-trench, sleeping at night in one of the bomb-bays, up at dawn trying to spot the unknown killers and encouraging his men constantly. He tried to give the impression of being a cool hand, never putting his head up at the same spot twice, ears and eyes always on the alert, but never allowing his men to notice the precautions he was taking as he moved up and down the trench, a permanent smile fixed on his thin face.

But it was no use. Twice he had been on the spot moments after a sentry had been shot and had surveyed the shell-shattered earth to their front. Nothing! In despair he had personally commanded the mortar team which had finally managed to destroy the mysterious concrete pipes which Captain Heinze had first spotted. Again it had been purposeless. One hour later, the sergeant in charge of the mortar team had been shot neatly through the back of the head, as he supervised the removal of the great clumsy mortar.

'*Heaven, arse and cloudburst, Pill!*' he had exploded to the MO that evening as they sat together in the medical dugout, smoking their pipes and sipping hot tea laced with rum, 'the bastards are making me an old man before my time! Three solid days I've been up there in the fire-trench now and not a sight of the bastards. You would think no-man's land is deserted for kilometres around and yet they're out there, picking off my poor chaps as easy as snapping your fingers.' He struck the rough packing-case table in front of him angrily with his clenched fist. 'There seems to be nothing I can do.'

The Pill looked at the younger man, his face hollowed out to an angry death's head in the flickering light of the candles stuck in empty schnaps bottles. 'I'll concede, Horst, that Friend Ivan is a past master of camouflage. We've seen it all before. They are our superiors at the nasty business of sniping. But snipers are human beings too, you know. To use the soldiers' phrase, they don't exactly shit through their ribs!'

Von Dietz shook his head gloomily. 'Don't think I haven't thought of that, Pill,' he said. 'I've checked for their waste products and any sign of smoke which might indicate they're heating food, for it must be devilishly cold for them out there without hot food. But nary a sign. They're the Red Army's elite. They survive on a handful of cold food and a sip of cold tea. And they hide their faeces like a cat does. No, that's not the answer, Pill.'

The doctor waited patiently until he had finished and said, 'I didn't exactly mean that, Horst.'

'What did you mean then?'

'This. They don't snipe at night, do they?'

'No.'

'So, what do you think they do during the hours of darkness?' The Pill answered his own question. 'I hardly think it's likely they stay in their freezingly cold burrows for the twelve or so hours of darkness. They wouldn't survive long if they did. Even the hardiest of our chaps can't stand much more than two hours at one go at night on sentry duty. So —'

'So,' von Dietz beat him to it, a light of hope beginning to dawn on his lean face, 'they crawl back to their own lines to sleep and eat, coming back before dawn with,' he added bitterly, 'Renewed strength and energy to murder our poor fellows.'

'Exactly. Well, Horst, don't you think that is the way?'

'You mean, root them out when they attempt to make their way back to their own lines?'

The Pill shook his head. 'No, I think they'll be too clever for that. They'd spot any patrol leaving our lines. That would only mean further casualties.'

Von Dietz's face lit up. 'You mean... Of course, when they're coming back?'

'Right,' the Pill's face lit up too. 'When they start to crawl back in their burrows for another day's killing, there will be a little reception committee waiting for them ... and that invitation will never be repeated.'

The CO nodded slowly. 'I agree, Pill. It will be a onetime invitation only...'

CHAPTER 6

When von Dietz had asked for volunteers almost as one the men of the First Battalion, which was on 'stand-down' that day, had stepped forward. For all of them hated the unknown snipers.

Von Dietz had smiled. 'Thank you, soldiers. I am proud of you.' For a few moments he had looked the length of the men standing to attention in the trench before making his decision. 'Ensign von Doerr, I shall take you and the first six men to your right, starting from Senior Soldier Deltgen.'

Now he and Ensign von Doerr's men made their preparations for the night's work, as the sky grew progressively darker and the evening lull started to descend upon the Leningrad Front.

Purposefully they blackened their faces and removed all badges of rank in case any one of them was unlucky enough to be captured. Each man stuck stick grenades down the sides of his boots and armed himself with the weapon of his choice, instead of the usual rifle. Most of them picked a pistol and all thrust a razor-sharp blackened bayonet down the side of their belts. Finally they drew on the ankle-length fur coats, normally issued for sentry-duty only, and pulled the flaps of their forage caps down about their ears, tying them under their chins. It was going to be a long, cold wait and Colonel von Dietz did not want to run the risk of their ears becoming frostbitten.

'A real bunch of gangsters,' he said, as he inspected them, noting that hoar-frost was already beginning to glitter on their forage caps. It certainly was going to be a very cold night. 'Now, utter silence, remember. But once we find a likely spot to wait for Friend Ivan, I want each man of you to work with his mate to ensure that neither of you falls asleep. That's a certain way of getting frostbite.' He favoured their earnest faces with a thin smile and said, 'Thank you, men. And if we pull this off, I promise each one of you twenty-four hours leave to the rear.'

Deltgen winked delightedly at Red Rudi. 'Women,' he said happily, and formed a circle with the forefinger and thumb of his thickly gloved right hand, to make his meaning quite clear.

But Red Rudi was not impressed. Instead he thrust up his own middle finger and growled surlily, 'Sit on that, you stupid Rhenish shit!'

Von Dietz flung a last look at the sky. It was dark enough and the moon had not yet risen. 'All right,' he whispered, 'off we go — and keep it quiet. We don't want to scare 'em — *just yet.*'

It was fortunate for them that the terrain was so difficult and their progress slow for otherwise they would have walked straight into the cunning little minefield planted just to the right of the shelled area. Fortunately, it was von Dietz himself who stumbled across the thin rabbit wire stretched across the snow. He had fallen to his knees and as he righted himself his fingers brushed across the prong jutting out of the snow.

'*Halt!*' he hissed instinctively. '*For God's sake nobody move!*'

'What is it, sir?' Ensign von Doerr just behind him asked urgently.

'Mines!' the tall CO answered, feeling a cold finger of fear trace its way down his spine.

'Shit!' Red Rudi cursed. 'Trapped in a shitting minefield in the middle of the shitting night.' As always the soldier with a shock of red hair was too angry even to be afraid. 'I allus like to get me jollies like this.'

'Shut up!' von Dietz snapped without rancour, for he valued the steadfastness of old heads like Rudi. 'We're not trapped yet. Now this is what we do. I go first and find the way through, then,' he took off his mitten and reached in his pocket to take out the luminous white tape, 'I'll play this out. You'll follow me at five metre intervals between each man — and remember I want you to walk *exactly* on the tape, otherwise …' he left the rest of his sentence unsaid.

'God in heaven!' Ensign von Doerr quavered fearfully. Behind him, Deltgen said reassuringly, 'Nothing to it, sir. Last time we were out, we were running into minefields all the time. Yer just got to concentrate, sir, that's all. And if you don't, well, try to make a handsome corpse.'

In the darkness von Dietz grinned. He wondered just how reassuring that particular statement was for poor scared von Doerr. Then his grin vanished and he commenced the operation.

Carefully he stepped over the wire which marked the edge of the little minefield and put his right foot down carefully, very carefully. Gingerly he brought his left foot up and stood there with his legs pressed close together, feeling the sweat spring up unpleasantly all over his body, in spite of the freezing cold. Nothing! He drew a deep breath and took another step forward, reeling out the glowing white tape as he did so. The minutes passed. Now he was about five or six metres into the minefield. Behind him he sensed the first man cross the rabbit wire, too. 'Follow the tape exactly,' he hissed and started once more, sweating like a pig, hardly daring to breathe, testing out the surface of the snow pace by pace.

Again the minutes passed in leaden apprehension, each fresh step made only by sheer will power after what seemed an eternity of deliberation, von Dietz's heart beating like a trip-hammer, his breath coming in short, hectic gasps.

Then it happened! He felt the scrape of metal against metal, as something scratched along the nailed surface of his boot. His first instinct was to withdraw his foot immediately. He caught himself in time, and paused there awkwardly, boot sole resting lightly against the plunger of the mine he knew to be there. 'Listen,' he said, fighting to keep his voice under control, 'who's behind me?'

'Deltgen, sir.'

Von Dietz breathed a small sigh of relief that it wasn't von Doerr; he would have lost his head immediately. 'Listen, Deltgen,' he said, 'my right boot is resting on the plunger of a mine.'

Behind him he heard someone gasp with fear and guessed it was the Ensign. He ignored the sound and continued, 'I want you Deltgen to work your way to me, kneel on the tape directly behind my left foot and uncover the thing. Got it?'

'Got it, sir.' Deltgen's Rhenish sing-song seemed no different than normal and again von Dietz blessed the fact that it was Deltgen; if anyone could carry out the difficult operation in the darkness, it would be Deltgen.

'All right, come now.'

'Said — done, sir! I'm on my way.'

And then Deltgen was at his feet, chin pressed against the calf of his left leg, gloves off, fingers boring into the snow, brushing it away from the top of the mine, giving a hushed running commentary as he worked. 'Wooden mine... Thank Christ it ain't magnetic with all the gear we've got on us... Feeling underneath now ... no wires so far ... no booby trap.'

'Check for a matchbox-fuse beneath it,' von Dietz croaked, the tension getting to him, sweat dripping from his brow now and blinding him. 'Might be attached to another…'

He couldn't say any more.

But Deltgen seemed as unconcerned as ever. 'No matchbox, sir … it's on its own … It can be lifted, sir, when you say the word.'

Von Dietz swallowed hard, knowing that now the most dangerous part of the operation had arrived. 'You know the drill, Deltgen, but I'll tell you once again. Once I lift my foot from the plunger the ugly thing will explode. So we'll have to lift together, you taking it out of the earth, I keeping my foot on the plunger. When —' *if*, a malicious little voice at the back of his mind interjected, but he ignored it, 'you've got it out, tell me. I'll lift my foot and in that very same moment fling it to our front.' In a strangled voice, he added, 'All of you drop at that moment. Clear?'

'Clear.'

'All right, then, Deltgen, let's get to it!'

In the darkness he heard the soldier give a sharp intake and knew why. One slip, one wrong move and both their bodies would be ripped to shreds by the dozen or so metal balls the mine contained. Split-second timing was essential.

'I'm lifting, sir.'

Together with Deltgen, von Dietz raised his foot, still keeping his sole resting on that plunger, the sweat pouring down his body, desperately trying not to lose contact, as the soldier eased the deadly mine out of the snow, listening to the scrape of the snow against it, body tense and expectant.

'Out,' Deltgen croaked after what seemed an eternity.

Von Dietz fought to keep himself from shouting. 'I shall count up to three, Deltgen, then you throw.'

'Sir.'

'*One* ... *two* ... *three.*' Von Dietz's voice broke completely as he screamed 'DUCK' and flung himself face-forward in a shallow dive into the snow.

Deltgen threw the mine forward in a low lob and cowered behind a prostrate von Dietz, head huddled in his arms, as with a thick crump the mine exploded. The horizon erupted with scarlet flame. Bits of steel shrapnel and metal balls hissed through the air. Something struck von Dietz a glancing blow on his helmet. For a moment or two, he thought he was going to black out, then he pulled himself together as from the Soviet line a machine gun started to chatter wildly. Tracer, a hissing red and white, cut the darkness frantically. He clambered to his feet, telling himself that if there had been other mines, the one thrown by Deltgen would have exploded them, and cried, 'Damn the mines — run for it. *Follow me, men!*' He started to pelt forward to where the snow was ringed with steaming fresh brown earth. 'Come on,' he cried over his shoulder, as his shaken men still hesitated, 'come on, you sons-of-whores, you don't want to live for ever, do you!'

Sobbing with fear, they raced after their CO, while the signal flares started to sail into the air over the Soviet lines and the machine-gun swung back and forth, seeking victims. But that was not to be — this night.

Five minutes later the whole bunch of them, chests heaving, lungs wheezing like ancient leather bellows, were squatting in a neatly made pit beyond the minefield, aware from the sweet smell of wood charcoal still coming from the big holed can that rested in its centre that they had found the snipers' nest...

CHAPTER 7

It was a terrible night. All but the cold now forgotten they huddled together, blue-lipped and teeth chattering with the icy cold. For a while the little can of charcoal threw off a little warmth, but about midnight the last of its heat vanished. Some of them tried to sleep in an attempt to forget the tremendous cold. But sleep was impossible too. The frost was like a poisonous reptile wriggling in through the gaps in their thick outer clothing, biting at their toes, creeping insidiously up their backs and arms, turning their poor bodies into miserable shaking hulks.

Von Dietz started to pray for the night to end. His joints ached with the cold. It seemed to congeal his blood and kill the very marrow of his bones. It was impossible. Even the occasional, frightening burst of machine-gun fire was welcome; it started the adrenaline working again for a few moments and brought a fleeting warmth to his poor frost-racked limbs.

At about five, in that pre-dawn period when he knew the front on both sides began to stir, he roused his sullen, miserable men and made them work their limbs the best they could in the cramped conditions of the pit. Then, he ordered each man to eat his bar of precious ration chocolate to give himself new energy before allowing them a sip from his flask of vodka. 'Pepper vodka,' he whispered, 'one sip per man. Now remember that,' he croaked hoarsely, as he handed it to Red Rudi.

'Holy strawsack,' the Berliner said thickly, 'I can die happy, pepper vodka!' Trying to contain himself, he raised the precious flask to his lips and allowed a few drops of the burningly hot alcohol to trickle over his parched tongue down his throat into his gullet where it exploded immediately and sent fire, beautiful fire, coursing through his frozen limbs.

Von Deitz waited until they had all had a sip before speaking. 'All right, it can't be much longer now, lads. I know it's been a hellish night — and I'll make it up to you once we get back to our own lines. But we've got to be alert, exceedingly alert, because we can assume that Friend Ivan will come back to his nest, with renewed energy and after a good night's sleep in a warm bed.'

'But how do we know this *is* the place, sir?' Ensign von Doerr objected.

'The can, the fact that this is a man-made hole and nobody digs a pit like this unnecessarily with the earth like iron, and that minefield back there. It could serve no tactical purpose whatsoever. Its only function is to protect Friend Ivan from any unwelcome surprise visitors. All right?'

'Yessir.'

'Now,' von Dietz continued, 'this is the drill. We could kill Friend Ivan when he makes his appearance.'

'I should think so,' Red Rudi growled, 'the Popov shits have killed enough of our fellers.'

'Agreed. But if we killed them, they would only be replaced by other snipers. No, Friend Ivan has the soul of a peasant — superstitious and easily frightened of things he doesn't understand. So, let's give him something to be frightened about.'

'How do you mean, sir?' Deltgen enquired.

'Well, let us just make his snipers disappear. Keep him guessing what has happened to them. Perhaps that might be a more effective way of keeping Friend Ivan off our backs for the rest of the time we're in the line here.'

The men considered the suggestion for a few moments, while to their front there came the faint rattle of mess tins as the Russian soldiers presumably lined up to receive that thick oatmeal soup they usually ate for breakfast.

'Sounds all right to me, sir,' Red Rudi admitted grudgingly. 'But how we gonna capture the Popovs alive, sir?'

'Like this. Assuming that they are experts, which they are, they'll head in the general direction of their nest here. All the same, I think they'll take precautions. So I want an alternative position ready for them just in case they get wind of us.' He looked at von Doerr, his face a white blur in the receding darkness. 'Ensign, I want you to take two men and position yourself to our right, over there near that clump of shattered firs.'

'But that's one hundred metres closer to their lines, sir,' von Doerr quavered, not attempting to conceal his fear now.

'Exactly, von Doerr,' von Dietz answered drily. 'This morning you're going to start earning your pay for the first time. You'll take up your positions there. If in any way Friend Ivan gets cold feet and begins to move back,' von Dietz's voice hardened, 'you are to stop him ... and I want no excuses. All right, off you go.'

Von Doerr muttered something but in the end he slithered out of the hole and set off, bent double, as if he expected to be hit by an enemy bullet at any moment, followed by two other soldiers.

Von Dietz waited until he was clear before he continued with, 'The rest of you better get into position now, too. But remember, no shooting unless it's absolutely necessary. Clear?'

'Clear, sir,' the others answered dutifully.

Now the faint sounds coming from the Russian lines — coughs, an occasional laugh, the rattle of tins, someone trying to start a stubborn motor in the freezing air — indicated that they were all wide-awake. The knowledge that soon the hated and feared snipers would come crawling out to start another day of sudden death made the waiting men forget the cold. They were all alert and in the case of Ensign von Doerr very tense. He knew why the CO had picked him for this outpost duty; it was to be a test of his nerves, and even now his forehead was cold with an anxious sweat. Could he bear the strain?

The minutes ticked away. Over at the Soviet lines a white flare hissed into the sky and momentarily threw their front into stark harsh relief.

Von Doerr swallowed hard. 'What's that?' he hissed, pointing ahead with a gloved hand that trembled violently, as the flare sank to the ground.

The man next to him chuckled. 'Nothing, Ensign, except the branch of a tree.'

Von Doerr croaked. 'But I thought it was an upraised arm.'

'It's always the same just before dawn, you can imagine all sorts of things, Ensign,' the old head said calmly.

Von Doerr mopped his streaming brow. For an instant he had thought it had been an upraised arm, its bent fingers coming to seize him.

Again time passed leadenly, as the sky began to flush the first dirty-white of the false dawn and over at the Russian line someone started to sing in a deep sad bass, as if the unknown singer bore all the sorrows of the world on his shoulders.

'Christ,' the old head grumbled, 'what's that lot of Popovs got to shittingly well sing about, I ask myself? They're just in the same...' He broke off suddenly and a petrified von Doerr could feel the man tense at his side.

'For God's sake, what is it?' he hissed in alarm.

'There's somebody coming...' The man next to him peered into the twilight gloom. 'I can definitely see somebody ... it's them!'

'Where?' von Doerr said, gripping the other man's left arm like a frightened child.

'Let go of me flipper, sir... Over there at eleven o'clock.'

Von Doerr spun his head round, feeling the small hairs standing erect with fear at the back of his neck, his lower body shaking uncontrollably. His heart seemed to stand still. The old head was right; there was a white-clad shape moving cautiously towards them, shoulders bent under what appeared to be a heavy camouflaged pack so that he looked like a hunchback. Behind him a second later a similarly clad figure appeared.

'His mate, sir,' the old head whispered out of the side of his mouth. 'One shit to spot and the other to shoot.' He chuckled softly. 'Well, they won't be doing much spotting once they land in the CO's hands, will they, sir?'

Von Doerr ignored the comment. The Russians were heading straight towards the little copse of shattered trees where they were hiding. Unless they deviated their present course they would bump straight into them!

Transfixed like a rabbit faced by a deadly snake, feeling his hands cramped desperately around the butt of his pistol, his chest heaving convulsively, von Doerr croaked, 'But they'll see us... We can't let them get any closer... They'll... they'll ... *kill us!*' He got those terrifying words out with a strange strangled twist of his head as if the breath was already being choked out of him. '*Kill us, do you hear!*'

'In God's name, sir,' the old head hissed urgently, 'keep it down! They'll hear us in a minute and bolt for it!... You know what the CO said, sir?'

But von Doerr was too terrified; now he was beyond all reason. 'They're coming for us!' he screamed. 'I must stop them! *I must!*'

Before the old head could stop him, von Doerr had risen to his feet. Fifty metres away the first of the snipers came to a sudden halt, and crouched, his surprise evident. Von Doerr raised his pistol, just as the sniper became aware of his danger and started to fumble with his rifle. More by good luck than good judgement, von Doerr loosed off the first shot. The sniper screamed and then started to give way at the knees making eerie gurgling sounds. It was too much for von Doerr. He dropped his pistol. '*I've had enough … I've had enough … I can't go on like this!*'

'*Sir!*' the old head bellowed and rose to his feet. '*You can't —*' He never finished the sentence.

The second sniper was quicker off the mark than his dying companion. He fired from the hip without aiming. The old head howled with pain. Next moment he pitched face-forward in the snow and lay perfectly still, while a screaming von Doerr ran for the rear, heedless of the fire-fight which had now commenced, tearing off his equipment as he bolted, overcome by a great, overwhelming fear…

'In three devils' name, why did you do it, Doerr?' Colonel von Dietz snapped, taking his eyes off the second sniper who Red Rudi and Deltgen dragged feet-first through the snow, too angry to be surprised by the fact that the body was that of a woman.

Von Doerr continued to blubber, the tears streaming down his ashen face. He did not answer.

'What a waste of good woman, sir,' Deltgen said with false heartiness, trying to defuse the tension. 'I had a feel of her tits when I lifted her up. By Christ each tit must have weighed a kilo! Fancy getting yer head between lungs like that…' His voice trailed away to nothing. No one was listening to him. All attention was focused on the sobbing officer, the tell-tale dark patch at the front of his trousers indicating that he had wet himself.

'Didn't you hear me?' von Dietz rapped, as the two soldiers let the feet drop.

Again the Ensign did not answer.

Beside himself with rage, von Dietz drew back his hand and slapped the sobbing man squarely across the face.

One of the greenbeaks gasped and von Doerr shook his head suddenly as if he were coming out of a trance. 'What,' he asked stupidly, 'what did you say … Colonel?'

Von Dietz hit him again. The Ensign staggered back and would have fallen if Deltgen had not caught him in time. Von Doerr looked reproachfully at his CO, eyes liquid with hurt and pain, a thin trickle of blood curling down from his left nostril. 'You are under arrest,' von Dietz snapped. 'Senior Soldier Deltgen.'

'Sir!'

'You will guard the prisoner until we return to our lines.'

'But what is going to happen to me?' von Doerr gasped tearfully.

Von Dietz gave him one last contemptuous look. 'You … you will be brought before a court-martial on a charge of cowardice in the face of the enemy… All right, come on, let's get out of this mess before Friend Ivan spots us.'

Deltgen gave his prisoner a gentle nudge as they set off back to their own lines once more. 'Come on, sir,' he urged. 'We'd better be going.'

'Cowardice in the face of the enemy,' von Doerr whispered in an awed voice. 'But that means a sentence of death, Senior Soldier.' Sombrely Deltgen nodded his head and said, 'I'm afraid it does, sir…'

CHAPTER 8

The Pill was late getting to the court-martial, held in the biggest dugout in the supply line — deliberately. He was burdened enough with the sufferings of the men of the 69th (for when they were hurt or wounded they ceased to be soldiers for the most part, and it fell to him to comfort them and reason away their terrors); he did not want to add the fate of Ensign von Doerr to them. But the CO had insisted. Every officer not on duty was commanded to attend.

Now as he pulled the heavy sacking curtain aside and entered the packed dugout, he found it so full of blue cigarette smoke that he seemed to see the pale faces of those attending through a mist. There was von Dietz, arrogant face set and revealing nothing. Opposite him facing the panel of officers seated at an improvised table — a line of ration crates covered with a grey Army blanket — was Ensign von Doerr. He was cleanly shaven, his uniform tidy and complete save for his pistol belt which had been taken from him, his white, cracked lips pressed close together, and his gaze fixed unseeingly on the wall.

The Pill frowned and slipped down on top of an empty ammunition box next to Sanders, the grey-haired commander of the First Battalion to which the Ensign belonged. He shook his head and whispered out of the side of his mouth. 'He hasn't a chance. The poor young fool.'

'But he's so young, a mere boy,' the Pill objected.

Sanders shrugged and said nothing.

Now Major Globke, the regimental adjutant who was prosecuting, began to sum up his case speaking quietly and without anger, occasionally shuffling his papers in front of him as if he were nervous and wished to avoid the accused's gaze. 'I know the prisoner is very young and that he volunteered for active service when he was barely the legal age to do so. That, all of us have to take into account. But *meine Herren*, Ensign von Doerr comes of an old Prussian military family which has served the country and this Regiment loyally for over two hundred years. He must have known what to expect.' The Major paused and gave a dry little cough, covering his mouth with his fist as if he had bad front teeth and was attempting to hide them. 'All of us, as I would be the first to admit, are frightened when we go into action. It is something, this sudden death, the noise, the chaos, that one can never get accustomed to, regardless of how often one does it. But,' he raised his voice suddenly, 'an officer has a duty — indeed, a sacred duty — to conceal that fear from his men. If he does not, they break down, everything breaks down. It is the end.' For the first time the Major looked directly at the pale youth in front of him. 'Ensign von Doerr did not conceal that fear. He let it get the better of him. The result was the failure of the regimental plan and the death of a good soldier — needlessly. *Meine Herren*, I demand the death penalty.' Abruptly he sat down and started playing with his papers again, leaving a heavy brooding silence to settle over the underground court.

The Pill flashed a look at von Dietz. There was no change in the look on his face and for the first time in his twenty-five years in the Army the Pill realized just how heavy the responsibility of command was. Horst was a sensitive man — he knew that. He was not demanding the death of this young man lightly, maliciously. The prospect, he knew, moved Horst, too. Yet the Regiment, in his mind, was more important than the life of one young man; for the Regiment represented the lives of three thousand young men.

Now it was the turn of the defending officer, Captain Diefenbach, Sanders' second-in-command, and the Pill could see immediately that his heart wasn't in the task before him. Not that he disliked his client, it wasn't that, the MO told himself. It was simply that he could think of no plausible argument to excuse von Doerr's conduct. Men might join the army because of idealism and patriotism, but they soon learnt that the wearing of the uniform betokened hard bondage and duty: a duty which demanded that the individual forget his individualism and at all times obey implicitly. Ensign von Doerr had infringed that unwritten rule and he would have to pay for it. In the end the defending officer ended with a lame, 'Gentlemen, I hope you will take into consideration the fact that Ensign von Doerr is a war volunteer ... and barely eighteen years of age.' He stopped and looked at the court a little red-faced, as if he felt he should say more, but not knowing exactly what. Abruptly he sat down.

The panel of officers did not take long to deliberate. The Pill wasn't surprised. Since the defeats of the summer and the increasing number of desertions and refusals to fight, the *High Command* had ordered that all such cases should be punished rigorously.

The President rose after a brief five minutes of discussion, ran his hand through his thinning grey hair and looked around at the silent officers present with a tired expression, as if he felt himself constrained to explain his decisions to them rather than the prisoner now standing rigidly to attention.

'There can be no war without casualties, gentlemen,' he said. 'That's war. Those casualties can be of two kinds — physical and emotional. Ensign von Doerr is an emotional casualty of his first battle. I understand that and I also take his age into account.' The President paused as if he were having difficulty in formulating his words and his listeners tensed expectantly, for now, most of them knew, he would pronounce the sentence. He had given his justification for his own conduct; now would come the punishment. The Pill said a silent prayer, knowing even as he said it, that it would not be granted.

'Be that as it may,' the President continued, 'but Ensign von Doerr is an officer and officers of the Greater German Army are not allowed to become emotional casualties.' Without looking at the tense, ashen-faced young man standing before him, he ended in a rush, 'The sentence of the court is that Ensign von Doerr should be executed by firing squad for cowardice in the face of the enemy. Take the prisoner away.'

The taller of von Doerr's two escort officers nudged the boy gently in the ribs, 'Come on, von Doerr, let's go,' he said softly.

Without a protest, the Ensign turned about and let himself be led away.

Colonel von Dietz waited till the blackout curtain had closed behind the prisoner, then he rose to his feet. 'Thank you, gentlemen,' he said and touched his hand to his cap as his officers sprang to their feet.

The Pill caught up with him as he stalked along the supply trench, seemingly unaware of the shocked looks on the faces of the men working there, who had obviously already heard of the sentence passed on the Ensign. 'Horst,' he said urgently, keeping up with him, 'you can still do something.'

'Do something?' von Dietz echoed, saluting automatically as his men clicked to attention, not looking at the doctor at his side.

'Yes, it is still an internal affair. Old Harz, the President of the Court, will do as you tell him, and the papers won't be forwarded up to Division till this evening when the rations come up. There's still time.'

'Time for what?' von Dietz said icily, noting that there seemed to be more activity over Leningrad than usual. The little wooden Russian spotter biplanes were everywhere in the hard-blue winter sky.

'Time to have von Doerr sent to — say — a punishment battalion or at the worst to Torgau.'

Von Dietz stopped in mid-stride and looked down at the doctor. 'Doctor Hartung,' he said with surprising formality, his voice cold and emotionless, 'Ensign von Doerr has been tried and found guilty by a properly constituted military court. They have passed the death sentence, not I. That is the end of the matter. Good day.' He touched his hand to his cap and strode off, leaving the Pill staring glumly at his boots...

'I don't like it,' Deltgen declared categorically, as he filled tracer bullets into a machine-gun belt under the watchful eye of the Bull.

'What don't yer like?' Red Rudi asked, as he did the same, ears humming with the *put-put* of the Soviet biplanes which were overhead.

'This business with von Doerr. They oughtn't to shoot him for that.'

'He's an officer, ain't he?' Red Rudi said as if that explained everything.

'He's only a lad, still wet behind the spoons. Bet he ain't even had it in yet — and tomorrow they're gonna blow his turnip off.'

The Bull lifted his face from the steaming hot cup of coffee, laced heavily with the rum one of his kitchen bull cronies had brought him, and said maliciously, 'Not *them* — *you*!' He grinned evilly.

Deltgen paused in his task and looked with feigned curiosity at his running-mate. 'Did you hear anybody speak, Rudi?' he asked.

'No,' Rudi answered equally innocently, 'it was one of the long-tails in yon dugout letting off a wet fart.'

The Bull was not offended. 'I'm shitting you not,' he said, pressing home his point, 'it's the First Battalion which will have to provide the firing squad for the yeller shit. Army tradition, you know. The soldiers who witnessed the offence have got to see the offender punished. Twelve men will be picked from the Battalion by Major Sanders and each one handed a round. Only one round will be live.'

Deltgen frowned. 'Are you sure that's what they do, Bull?' he said. 'And none of yer shit now.' He raised his gloved fist, 'Or else some big fat bastard of a noncom is gonna get a knuckle-sandwich right smartish.'

The Bull's smirk vanished. 'Honest, Deltgen,' he said hastily. 'That's the way they do it... I was on a firing squad before the war of a squaddie who raped a kid when we marched into Austria. So I know.' Hastily he bent his head over his cup of coffee.

Deltgen looked at Rudi, and said, 'I for one am *not* going to do it, and that's that!' Savagely he slipped another cartridge into the belt of machine-gun ammunition...

The news that the First Battalion was to provide the firing squad passed from dugout to dugout that evening. Squatting on their straw, scratching at the lice, their faces worn and unshaven in the flickering lights provided by the candles, the men, old heads and greenbeaks alike, discussed the possibility that they might be selected by Major Sanders for the firing squad which would shoot Ensign von Doerr at dawn. Even the unusual rumble of guns that came from the Soviet positions and the squeaky rattle of tracks that indicated there were gun-tractors about somewhere were forgotten.

'It's not right,' they said. 'Why should we be forced to shoot him? If they want him shot, let them do it themselves — or bring in those shits of head-hunters . Why should we do their dirty work for them, eh?'

'It's only a lad,' they said. 'Just because he's an officer, they're gonna line him up against a wall and blast the crap out of him. We'd probably have done the same in his position. It's a shitting awful shame!' And they said, 'I'm not gonna do it anyway, if I'm picked. I'm likely to be the one that gets the real bullet. I couldn't have that on my conscience. *No, not me!*'

And as the candles grew ever lower and the sound of the squeaky tracks died away, the bitter talk gave way to furtive conspiratorial whispers, which silenced whenever a senior noncom or officer appeared at the door of the dugouts. The very air seemed thick and heavy with plotting.

Colonel von Dietz could not sleep. He lay on his back on his plank-bunk, listening to the tip-tap of the machine-guns and the creaking rumble of the guns at the Front and watching the flame of the candle flicker every now and again with their vibrations.

His soul rebelled against what he was going to have witness done on the morrow. Could he stand the looks on the stolid, good-humoured faces of his men who would see this judicial murder? It would be the end to the innocence of many of them. They were bound to be harder, more brutal men afterwards. It was inevitable.

Yet it had to be done. The honour and future of the Regiment demanded it.

'*The Regiment?*' that harsh little voice at the back of his mind said cynically, 'is that all you think about? Isn't there anything else left of your life now — but the damned 69th? But what have I left but the Regiment?' he countered within himself, his eyes suddenly filled with despair. 'Family, honour, my Fatherland, run by madmen and criminals — they're all gone. A man *has* to have something to which he can cling surely!'

But the voice was silent, and Colonel von Dietz, alone on that long cold winter's night with the guns rumbling ominously outside, was left with his thoughts. They were not pleasant.

CHAPTER 9

Dawn. A chill wind blew across the snowfield, wreathing the feet of the eight hundred men drawn up in a hollow square with a fog of snow, so that they appeared to be floating there. In the skeletal black trees, silhouetted harsh and stark against the grey wintry sky, the rooks cawed hoarsely. Nobody spoke, nobody moved, in spite of the freezing cold. Somehow it didn't seem right to do so. All eyes were fixed on the fresh stake of wood that had been driven overnight into the frozen snow and the backstop behind it formed by an armoured car. To their rear at the front the Soviet guns continued to rumble, the ever-present background music to war.

There was the wheeze and creak of a captured Russian truck coming slowly across the rutted snowfield. It came to a stop just outside the square. The Bull got out of the driver's cab. Even he seemed subdued and somehow smaller this cold dawn, as he slapped his gloved paw against the canvas of the back and said, 'All right, everybody out!'

Reluctantly, although they had just come from the best breakfast they had had for weeks and had been given a glass full of schnaps too, the firing squad dropped to the snows, refusing to look at the waiting First Battalion, as if they were ashamed of themselves for some reason or other. Led by Deltgen and Red Rudi, who held their rifles with distaste, they filed into position.

A few minutes later, Ensign von Doerr, escorted by two officers, made his appearance, his hands tied behind his back, his face pale but composed. The officers led him to the stake and one of them produced a rope to bind his hands to it. He shook his head and they didn't. Instead one of them pinned the white paper heart to his thin chest above the spot where the real organ was located. There was a gasp from the watching First Battalion, and a soldier fainted. Angrily the Bull snapped, 'Get that sissy shit out of here — quick!' They waited. Over Leningrad the sky was pink with explosions, but no one had eyes for the beleaguered city; all attention was focused on the victim standing there against the stake, staring into nothingness while his escorting officers smoked moodily, the thin blue smoke of their cigarettes rising stiffly into the still, cold air.

Finally the little car bearing von Dietz and the President of the Court rattled up. Sanders called the Battalion to attention, and dressed in full uniform, complete with ceremonial sword, the President hurried forward to the centre of the square. He cleared his throat and started hastily to read out the sentence, as if he wanted to get the unpleasant task done and finished with, his words punctuated by the increasing firing from the Soviet lines. 'The sentence is death,' he concluded and backed away, while the young officer in charge of the firing squad marched crisply over the frozen snow to take up his position.

Von Doerr's escorts looked at him. He nodded wanly. They, too, marched off.

Now all was tense silence in the rigid square of helmeted soldiers save for the cawing of the rooks in the trees.

The officer in charge of the firing squad licked his lips and the Pill standing next to von Dietz, whose face revealed nothing, could see just how nervous he was. 'Firing Squad,' he commanded, his breath fogging on the cold air, 'firing squad — *port arms*!'

There was a moment's hesitation and then the twelve soldiers went through the drill movements rigidly till they had their weapons in the correct position across their greatcoated chests. The Pill felt his brow go damp with sweat. The tension now was almost unbearable.

The officer raised his voice again. 'Squad,' he commanded, his voice shrill, as if he, too, was finding the tension too much for him, '*take aim!*'

Again there was a moment's hesitation before the firing squad brought up their rifles in the same measured disciplined manner and pointed them at the lone figure standing there in front of the stake.

The officer in charge raised his officer's dagger high above his head. Here and there men of the First Battalion gasped with shocked anticipation, and the Pill noticed a sickly-looking boy with glasses closing his eyes as if he couldn't bear to watch. The dagger came down in a silver gleam and the officer cried, '*FIRE!*' his face suddenly red with the effort.

Nothing happened!

For what seemed an age, the young officer stared at the men of the firing squad who poised there, their rifles tucked deep into their right shoulders, as if he couldn't believe the evidence of his own eyes, perhaps wondering if he had actually given the order to fire. Then he flashed a helpless look at his Battalion Commander, Major Sanders.

An urgent whispering broke out in the ranks of the First Battalion, but the Bull was too shocked by what had just happened to stop it. It started to grow in volume, as Major Sanders took a pace forward and cried, 'Friderichs, give the order to fire again!'

'Sir,' the young officer snapped, grateful for the support. He raised his dagger once more and said, 'Firing squad — take aim!' Hardly waiting for them to do so as regulations prescribed, he commanded, '*FIRE!*'

Again nothing happened and suddenly Red Rudi, his face a mixture of fear and anger, let his rifle sink. The gesture acted as a signal to the rest of the firing squad. One by one they did the same, while the officers of the First Battalion gawped at them in open-mouthed stupidity.

The Bull gawped, his massive chest heaving as if he were in his death throes, meaningless sounds coming from his mouth, as he looked from the firing squad and then to Colonel von Dietz, whose face — alone of those present — showed no emotion whatsoever.

The officer in charge of the firing squad lowered his dagger slowly and said, his voice cracked and broken, 'Didn't you hear the order, men?'

Red Rudi looked at him coldly. 'We heard all right, Lieutenant,' he snarled.

'Well, why … why didn't you obey it?' the young officer stuttered incredulously.

'Because, sir,' Red Rudi answered, selecting his words with care and controlling his evil temper, for he knew on what very dangerous ground he was now treading, 'we don't think that young Ensign von Doerr should be shot.' He jerked his head in the direction of the condemned man, on whose face new hope was beginning to dawn. 'It wouldn't be fair.'

'It wouldn't be fair, did you say…? *Not fair*?'

All eyes turned to Colonel von Dietz who had spoken, his hand suddenly clapped to his pistol holster, his eyes blazing with menace. 'Since when have you been commanding the 69th Regiment of Infantry, man?'

Red Rudi seemed to stagger back physically under the lethal impact of that look. For what seemed a long time he couldn't find his voice, while von Dietz, taking his time (for he knew full well that if he made the wrong decision, he could lose his beloved Regiment), stalked to the centre of the square to face the sullen firing squad, hands on hips, legs spread apart, as he looked at them.

'I'm now going to give you an order,' von Dietz said slowly, running his gaze along the ranks of shame-faced men who could not meet his eyes. 'I shall say it once and once only.' He let the words sink in before adding, 'If that order is not carried out, I shall have every one of you arrested. The charge will not merely be disobeying but *mutiny*!'

Swiftly, hand still on his pistol holster, he marched to the side of the firing squad. Unnoticed by the tense watching soldiers, red signal flares started to rise along the whole length of the Soviet positions. For an instant the Pill could have sworn he could hear a military band playing, then he, too, was caught up by this taut little scene being played out before him.

Von Dietz clicked to attention. 'Firing squad,' he commanded harshly, 'take aim!'

Not a soldier moved. Instead they stared at their feet like hopeless, dumb, beaten animals.

Von Dietz did not hesitate. 'Sarnt-Major Bulle!' he cried at the top of his voice.

The Bull pulled himself out of his shocked bewilderment and bellowed back, 'Sir!'

'Bring a platoon and put these men under close arrest — *immediately*!'

'*Sir*!'

Von Dietz swung round and at a measured pace began to walk to where von Doerr stood, while the Bull readied his platoon. The Pill and the rest watched him, but perhaps of all those present, only the old doctor knew instinctively what the CO was going to do — *had* to do — soon. Outwardly, von Dietz seemed cold and aloof. Inwardly, the Pill knew, von

Dietz was occupied with an inner reality that centred on the Regiment, its long tradition, and the fact that if the Regiment fell apart, everything would do so. It would be the end of everything.

The Pill shivered and swallowed hard as von Dietz halted in front of von Doerr. He wanted to look away, but he forced himself to keep his gaze fixed on the two men standing out there facing each other in silence, the one who would die soon and the one who would live a little longer.

Slowly, very slowly, von Dietz unbuttoned the flap of his holster and drew out his pistol. Behind him, the Bull's platoon had disarmed the firing squad, but still they had not moved off for they were too caught up in the tragedy which had now reached its final act.

The Pill watched the CO's lips move as he said something to the prisoner. Von Doerr's face was deathly pale, but the cowardice had vanished from his face and he held himself erect, even proudly. Slowly he nodded, as if in affirmation. Von Dietz backed off six paces, doing so formally, as if it were part of some old military ceremony. He raised his pistol. The Pill could see the knuckles of his hand whiten as he tightened his finger around the trigger. Von Doerr thrust back his head. '*Es lebe Deutschland!*' he cried in the same instant as the CO fired.

Next moment he was swung off his feet by the impact of a bullet at such short range and slammed to the ground, the front of his shirt suddenly flushed a bright crimson. Smoking pistol still in his hand, von Dietz hurried to him. The crowd waited. He bent down and felt the side of von Doerr's neck with his free hand. The Pill knew he was feeling for the artery. But there was no pulse. Gravely von Dietz pulled down the dead boy's eyelids, and straightened up, just as the alarm whistles and gongs started to sound and the first baleful elemental howl of the Soviet barrage ripped the dawn silence apart.

'*They're coming ... they're coming... The Ivans are coming...* !' the cries of alarm started to be heard on all sides. Abruptly the execution was forgotten and officers were bellowing orders frantically, while their men snapped off their safety catches and unslung their weapons.

THE   BATTLE   FOR   LENINGRAD   HAD COMMENCED...

BOOK TWO: *THE PIMPLE*

'Do not believe that soldiers get used to war and danger.
They never do.'
A Worden.

CHAPTER 1

Now there was new hope in the city.

The exhausted starved civilians still fell dead on the Neva Prospekt to lie there stiff and unheeded until the soldiers came to collect them, heaving them aboard the sledges like so many logs of wood. They still drank beer and vodka prepared from dried orange rind and ate Leningrad blockade-jelly, made from carpenter's glue. And they were still cut off save for what they called 'The Road of Life', which lay across the ice of Lake Ladoga, and cracked and fissured alarmingly every time the truck and motor sledge convoys rolled across it under the cover of darkness, bringing with them new supplies and fresh troops. But now there was hope again, for the Red Army was attacking once more after eighteen months of holding the line. From the ruined suburb of Kolpino, fresh troops, brought up secretly for the last month, were driving forward at Marshal Stalin's express order, to bring the German grip on the city to an end once and for all.

Now the great colonnades of the Bourse, the Winter Palace, the Admiralty which lay along the frozen River Neva echoed with the marching feet of thousands of men hurrying to the Front. The well-fed and confident units brought in from the Far East even sang; and the old women and men dragging their dead on sledges behind them to dump them in the Neva, if they could find an ice-free hole, stopped and stared in open-mouthed amazement. *People actually still sung!*

Now the citizens started to edge cautiously into Kazan Cathedral, and say their prayers with the frightened bearded priests who had survived the anti-religious purges of the thirties. Prayers of thanks that delivery seemed at last to be within sight.

Even the long-range German guns which would plant their tremendous shells near Griboyedov Canal or Uritsky Square no longer seemed so frightening, and people told each other, 'The Fritzes are no longer so accurate as they were. Their gunners are being driven back. Soon we'll be out of range altogether…' 'Yes,' others agreed in wan cheeked anticipation, their eyes seemingly feverish and bulging from their skull-like faces, 'once our armies link up outside to the west, then it will all be over and there will be food for all once again. Just let them link-up and then, comrades, the war is over for us up here in Leningrad!'

'The link-up, Comrade General,' Zhdanov grunted, and tugged at the end of his bulbous nose as if he were angry, 'that's all they can talk about up there on the surface — *link-up!*'

General Govorow, commander of the Leningrad Front, looked across the packing-case table littered with maps at the city's political leader. 'Your citizens have had a very tough time, Comrade. It's understandable. But we of the Leningrad Front and our comrades down there to the south of the Volkhov Front cannot perform miracles, you know. We are doing our best.' General Govorow stared through his rimless pince-nez at the burly balding political leader, who looked more like a village schoolmaster than the experienced officer he was.

'I understand, Comrade,' Zhdanov said, 'I understand. But you must understand the mood of those people up there too. I won't attempt to pull the wool over your eyes, Comrade General. There are many in the city who maintain that that gentleman in the Kremlin has deliberately made little effort to relieve us here because he has no liking for the Leningraders — and me.'

The General said nothing and hoped that his staff officers at the back of the great stone underground chamber had not heard that particular heresy. Stalin, the dictator in the Kremlin, had his spies everywhere, and the Gulag archipelago awaited all who offended him.

'I'm fighting for this city,' Zhdanov said vehemently. 'Not for Mother Russia, not for Stalin, not even for communism! I have had eighteen terrible months of siege here, comrade. The result is that I now know I am struggling — and my people too — for one thing only — *to save and free Leningrad*! Can you therefore not understand just how vital this link-up between your army and that of the Volkhov Front is?'

The big bespectacled General felt uneasy under the Commissar's scrutiny. It was too naked, too unashamed, too intense. Leaders, he told himself, should not look at each other like that; they should conceal their emotions. Those should be left to the common folk, the cannon fodder at the Front and the peasants. To hide his unease, he beckoned to the white-coated orderly and made the gesture of turning the tap of the great steaming brass samovar at the rear of the room. 'Tea, Comrade?' he said, as the orderly came hurrying up with the steaming glasses and the little jar of strawberry jam substitute, made from berries collected in Leningrad's parks. 'The tea at least is genuine,' he added, 'it came across the Lake last night.' He waited till Zhdanov had put a spoonful of the jam into his tea and then said, 'As you know, each night we are pouring men by their thousands across the Lake and supplies are coming in from other Fronts which need them just as urgently as the Leningrad one.'

Zhdanov raised his head from his glass, his thick nose now gleaming with moisture from the steaming tea, and grunted, 'Tell my people that, Comrade, when they're cooking the paste from the back of wallpaper into a gruel and boiling down leather for some kind of nourishment. While only kilometres away the Fritzes are guzzling fried eggs and potatoes and swilling them down with litres of real schnaps.'

The General raised his free hand, as if to ward off a physical blow from the disgruntled Commissar who squatted there in his shabby black fur-jacket, his boots wrapped in thick rags for extra warmth. 'All this we understand, Comrade,' he said hastily, 'and the link-up is only a matter of days. But there is one obstacle which we haven't yet overcome and which is proving difficult to eradicate.'

'What's that?'

'The Pimple.'

'The what?' Zhdanov exclaimed.

The General favoured him with a thin, cold smile. 'Well, that's what the Ivans at the Front call it. If you will be good enough to look at this chart.' He shuffled the maps on the packing-case table till he found the sector he was looking for. 'Look, here is Schlusselberg, the objective of the Volkhov Front and here — Sinyavino, our objective... Now, here to the south-west of those two is Height 560, the number indicates its height in metres.'

Zhdanov nodded, 'Yes, I know it from before the war. Go on.'

'It is the only physical feature of the whole Leningrad area of any great height and it — this is most important, Comrade — it dominates our Front. Even if we slipped around it, it would always present a danger to our flanks. It must be taken if we are to break the Fritzes' stranglehold on Leningrad.'

Zhdanov looked at the General blankly. 'Well take the damn place then!' he snapped.

'Take it?' Govorow laughed hollowly. 'But my dear Commissar —'

'Don't you damn well "dear Commissar" me!' the civilian interrupted crudely. 'I'm not red on the surface and damned bourgeois brown beneath when scratched like so many of your party bosses. I have no time for tea and fancy talk. I want action!'

'All right, Comrade,' the General answered, suddenly tight-lipped and flushed, 'I'll give it to you straight. I have already lost the equivalent of two and a half battalions in an attempt to seize the place in a *coup de main*. It just didn't work against the Fritzes' fixed defences, excellent soldiers, and the advantage they have on that damned Pimple of height. My reserves are not inexhaustible, you know, Comrade.'

'Then use armour,' Zhdanov replied unimpressed.

'*Armour*! By the Black Virgin of Kazan, Comrade, where am I supposed to get armour from? You know as well as I do that the ice on Lake Ladoga is too thin to support the weight of our T-34S.'

For the first time since he had entered the command bunker to urge the General to speed up his drive to link up with the Volkhov Front, Commissar Zhdanov smiled, his cunning little eyes almost disappearing into the folds of his broad red face, while the General stared at him, wondering at this sudden change of mood. 'What would you say, Comrade General,' the Commissar began slowly, 'if I were to promise you six T-34 tanks within the next forty-eight hours?'

'I would say that a miracle had occurred, Comrade, that is if one still believes in such religious nonsense.'

Zhdanov crossed himself with a cynical grin on his face, happy that he had been able to surprise the General. 'Then start believing. We'll be having you on your knees praying in Kazan Cathedral before long. Would you like to see them, Comrade General?'

All that the surprised General could do was nod his head, struck dumb by this exciting piece of news — tanks, if they were real, would transform the whole situation on the Leningrad Front!

Together in the General's motorized sledge, escorted by a troop of mounted Red Cossacks, they fought their way through the shoving, swirling crowd of infantrymen who had just crossed Lake Ladoga and were now forming up to march straight to the Front. Meanwhile the wounded, soldier and civilian, lay everywhere on blood-soaked stretchers in the freezing cold, waiting to be evacuated. Commissars everywhere were reading from their prepared texts, urging the soldiers to die for their Motherland, here and there attempting to get them to sing as they marched off, in order to encourage the emaciated civilian spectators. Someone was shouting a little desperately, *'Where's my rifle?... I can't go up the line without my rifle...'*

On they rode to the roar of the sledge-motor and the clip-clop of the cavalry's hooves, into the shattered suburb of Kolpino, which General Govorow knew had until recently been the frontline itself for many months. Now once again people milled about in the ruined, debris-littered streets and here and there, old women muffled in black, recognizing the Commissar waved to him as the sledge swept past. Dutifully he waved back, and said, 'Another month of the siege, General, and those poor old *babushkas* will no longer be alive. They probably haven't a gram of surplus body fat on them under all those clothes.' The General said nothing and wondered where in God's name the politician was taking him. The thunder of the guns was becoming louder by the minute and his own quick estimate told him somewhat alarmingly that they couldn't be more than five or six kilometres from the Front now. But finally the sledge came to a halt outside what appeared to be a ruined factory, its girders twisted into fantastic, grotesque shapes by the shelling, and what was left of its stark shattered walls pock-marked with shrapnel-holes like the symptoms of some kind of loathsome skin disease.

'The Izhrosky Industrial Plant,' the Commissar announced, pushing aside the rug which had covered his legs. 'We're here.'

'But what...' the General spluttered, unable to find the words he needed. 'The tanks ... the place is a ruin.' The Commissar grinned at his astonishment. 'General, follow me,' he said confidently, 'and all will be explained.' While the escort dismounted and stared in bewilderment around them at the piles of rubble and the sledge-driver hastily drove his vehicle to the shelter of the nearest wall in case the Fritzes had spotter planes out this morning, the Commissar led the General to what appeared to be a shattered workshop — broken lathes and benches lay everywhere among the rubble. He stopped at a huge door made of rough planking and knocked on it three times, while the General's bewilderment deepened by the second.

Finally it creaked open and a woman dressed in overalls and a sailor's cap stood there, her face delicate yet stern. In her dirty hands, she held a sub-machine gun.

'Can I pass, sentry?' the Commissar asked sternly, then his voice lightened. 'How is your man, Annya?'

'He died at the Front yesterday,' the sentry said tonelessly. 'Yes, you can pass.'

Together they entered and the plank door closed firmly behind them. Before them lay a long tunnel lit by naked low-watt bulbs. Now for the first time the General could hear the hum of machines and smell the heavy cloying odour of engine oil. 'What is this place?' he asked uneasily.

'As I told you — the Izhrosky Plant. Only since it was destroyed, it has gone below ground.'

'An underground factory?'

'Exactly. Come on. Let me show you.'

Together they walked down the sloping tunnel and swung open the metal door at its end. The noise hit them in the face with an almost physical blow. The vast cellar which lay before them was subdivided by heavy metal screens where hundreds of electric lathes hummed and rattled and tractor motors roared, generating electricity to run the lathes which were puffing and snorting like ancient samovars.

'*Boshe moi!*' the General roared above the tremendous clatter and din, watching a group of women milling something or other, their bodies wreathed in blue fiery sparks, their faces taut with the strain of the heavy work.

'Come,' Zhdanov cried, 'now I shall show you our pride and joy!'

Obediently the General followed the civilian through that great echoing cellar with its busy men and women, stinking of diesel oil, black tobacco, stale air and fumes. Then turning round another metal screen they saw them: Six T-34s, poised in the centre of a long shopfloor looking lithe — and deadly. 'But where ... where did you get them from?' he asked, hesitantly stroking the steel side of the nearest tank, noting as he did so the gleaming silver rut gouged in its flank where an anti-tank shell had struck.

'They were abandoned in the great retreat of autumn '41 by our people. Either because they had been hit or because they'd run out of fuel. It cost the factory the lives of fifteen men and four women to get them back here.' He nodded to the *brigadier* in charge who looked up briefly from a turret upon which he was painting a red star and then continued his work again. 'I have heard some people have saved a bottle of precious pepper vodka to celebrate the day when the siege of Leningrad is broken, we have saved these tanks for that purpose — to help end the siege.' He turned and flung General Govorow a bold challenging look. 'Comrade General, there they are. They will be yours in forty-eight hours. With them you will eradicate this ... er ... damned Pimple of yours and we will be free at last...'

CHAPTER 2

The dead man lay in the churned-up earth and broken timber, his arms stretched out stiffly as if he lay on a cross. It seemed somehow to Colonel von Dietz sacrilege to crawl over him, but he knew he had to if he wished to survey the ground below. Followed by the Pill, he crawled over the body, the weight causing blood to spurt from the terrible wounds. Von Dietz pinched his nostrils against the cloying, nauseating stench of fresh blood mixed with shell fumes.

It was now six days since the Soviets had attacked so surprisingly, and they had been ordered to take over Height 560 by a frantic divisional commander who saw his whole line crumbling under the massive enemy drive. Since then the 69th had been under constant bombardment combined with an all-out Soviet infantry attack, which had left the slope beneath them furrowed by steaming heaps of fresh brown earth and littered grotesquely with the bodies of Red Army infantrymen, so many of them that the snow appeared to be covered with an earth-brown carpet, the colour of their smocks.

Now the dawn-hate was over and the defenders huddled in their trenches above the two officers, their ears still full of the antiphonal elemental fury of that bombardment. Some staring at their hands in a state of catatonic fear; others hiding their heads in their greatcoats; a few joking or whistling hysterically; but all shaken, ashen-faced and numb with endurance.

The Pill crawled into the little shell-hole beyond the dead man and raised his binoculars too, carefully shading the glass with one hand so that no gleam from it might betray them to a sniper lurking out there in that devastated lunar landscape.

Together they surveyed the city lying below at some three or four kilometres' distance. They scanned the grey buildings, built two centuries before by Peter the Great's German architects and masons, appearing to cling to the side of the gleaming snake of the Neva; then they scanned the closer shattered cottages and more modern tenement housing that had once been that of the workers, but now, as they knew, was occupied by enemy troops. No movement could be seen — the whole front seemed to be deserted. Yet they knew the houses — or what was left of them — and their cellars were packed with enemy troops, their officers doing what they were doing — observing Height 560 through binoculars, planning the next attack.

'What do you think?' the Pill broke the heavy brooding silence disturbed only by the slow monotonous chatter of an old-fashioned enemy machine-gun to their right, its tracer hissing across no-man's land like a flight of red-hot angry hornets. 'Will they attack again this morning?'

'Yes,' von Dietz said quite casually. 'Only question is — where?' He took a final look at the positions below and said, 'Come on, let's back up into the trenches and see how the men are making out... My guess is that we've got about another hour before Friend Ivan decides to pay us another call.'

Once again they crawled over the crucified soldier, their nostrils filled with his nauseating stench, to drop into the nearest trench, packed with weary men. But slowly they were beginning to recover. Von Dietz could see that. They always did, he told himself, thank God! Their eyes had begun to take on that peculiar look which he knew so well, which marked them — old heads and greenbeaks — as veterans: a look which was strangely mature and worn, a kind of slow enduring energy. Under their rags and grotesque wrappings he knew that their bodies were lean and hard and somehow tireless.

Slowly he and the Pill started to pass down the line, stopping every now and again to have a word with a soldier or inspecting a section of trench, here and there looking at some of the men's feet at the MO's command; for the hospital bunkers were filled with wounded men and the Regiment did not want to lose men needlessly because of trench foot. In some cases when the soldiers removed their boots and socks big patches of skin stuck to them, and when the Pill saw the toes all white with blisters and the heels a dull crimson, he knew there was nothing for it but to order them to report sick. Otherwise he knew that one morning they would take off their socks to check their feet and their frostbitten toes would go with them.

In the end von Dietz and the Pill completed their tour and headed for the spot where the Bull supervised his kitchen-bulls. They were preparing the first hot food of the day on the last two remaining goulash-cannon (for the others had been destroyed in the terrible shelling of the first day of the Russian attack). 'Well Bulle,' von Dietz demanded as the big NCO, his face unshaven, eyes sunk and clearly revealing his own fear, forced himself to stand to attention, 'what's the food situation like?'

'Bean soup, sir, half a litre per man.'

Von Dietz frowned. 'Bread?'

Bulle shook his head.

'Chocolate … sugar?' he asked hopefully, knowing from experience that the men could forget the gnawing hunger pains for a while if they were given even as little as a spoonful of sugar.

Again the NCO shook his head. 'Last sack went yesterday, sir. Got a spoonful per head they did,' he added, conveniently forgetting that he and the kitchen bulls had gorged themselves on great handfuls of the precious white substance during the morning bombardment.

Von Dietz nodded sombrely and said to the Bull, 'I want volunteers to go out into no-man's land. There's a horse out there, a hundred metres or so from our wire. It'd provide at least a cube of meat per man if we could bring it in.'

'Volunteers, did you say, sir?' the Bull quavered, his hands beginning to tremble again at the very thought. His brain raced as he thought of some way of avoiding having to take part in an operation of that kind himself; for he knew why the CO had asked him. Nobody could be spared from the line; the volunteers would have to come from the kitchen bulls — and more frighteningly — himself. Then he had it. 'Sir, if I might make a suggestion?'

'Suggest away,' von Dietz said airily, trying to assess the number of white beans a soldier might get in half a litre of soup.

'The jail-bait, sir. Why not let them *volunteer*! They've done shittingly well nothing since the Popovs attacked except hide out in one of the dugouts.'

'You mean the firing squad?' von Dietz said, recalling the men he had placed under close arrest on that fateful day in what now seemed another age. 'I'd completely forgotten about them.' He sniffed. Over the Soviet lines the usual red flares were beginning to sail into the grey morning air, indicating that it would not be long before they attacked again. 'Do you think they'd volunteer?'

'Why not, sir?' the Bull asked, feeling pleased that he had got out of the nasty business himself. 'Offer them their release in exchange for volunteering. Then send them back to the line. Those stupid stubble-hoppers won't last long up there as it is.'

'Good idea,' von Dietz said after a moment's consideration. 'Tell any man who volunteers that the charges against him will be dropped. Now Sarnt-Major, get on with it. It won't be long now before Friend Ivan starts dropping some more square eggs on our heads. Come on, Doctor, let's move…'

'What do you think?' the Pill asked, passing von Dietz a tin cup, filled with surgical spirit mixed with water, for now all who could were drinking spirits most of the day and night; it was one way to forget the terror and misery of their position trapped on the Height.

Outside there was the first obscene thud and grunt of a mortar, as the Soviets opened up with their preliminary softening-up barrage prior to the infantry attacking yet again. Von Dietz took a sip of the fiery mixture and grimaced. 'Our position? Oh, Pill, we're in no dire trouble at the moment, save for supplies. It's hardly likely that Friend Ivan can bring up armour to winkle us out and I think we can continue to have the edge on his infantry. But,' he hesitated for a moment, as the dugout trembled under the impact of a near miss and the earth came tumbling down in a fine rain from the ceiling, and the place flooded with the acrid fumes of explosive, 'if our food and ammo run out, then we're in trouble, serious trouble.'

'A hypothetical question, Horst,' the doctor said, 'what would *you* do if that happened?' He grimaced as yet another mortar bomb exploded outside and set the earth vibrating like a living thing. 'I mean old Degenhardt at Division is an old woman. He wets his knickers at the slightest thing, but even he won't order a retreat unless the command comes from the FHQ itself. And you know the Führer. Every metre of earth is holy. It must be fought for to the last man and the last round, and all that sort of idiotic rubbish. Would you take the law into your own hands and face the consequences?' He looked hard over his tin cup at the younger man.

Von Dietz pondered the question while the world shook and quaked outside. He knew the rear-echelon swine of the Divisional staff. They had bath-houses, cinemas, canteens, officers' club, even Front-brothels. They moved around in a little tight pleasurable world of their own, far removed from the brutal realities of the Front, and they had no intention of losing those privileges by giving the wrong order. Their first loyalty would be to themselves and not to the Front swine of the 69th Regiment and its two sister regiments. 'I don't rightly know, Pill,' he said finally. 'As you say, I'd get no support or orders from Degenhardt on that score. It would be up to me. Then I suppose I'd be in the same position as those chaps with Deltgen who refused to shoot poor young von Doerr. How would it be regarded by the Führer HQ — cowardice perhaps? Even mutiny, the same crime as I accused the firing squad of.' He grinned suddenly and finished his drink. 'Somehow or other, I don't think I would get off as lightly as they are at this moment, dragging in a poor dead nag through no-man's land, do you?'

'I doubt it very much,' the Pill agreed finishing off his drink too, for the mortar 'stonk' had reached its furious crescendo now and the casualties would start pouring in soon; he had to be prepared. 'Well, let's hope that particular eventuality never occurs, Horst.'

'Yes, indeed,' von Dietz agreed, grabbing for his helmet as the whistles started to shrill once again along the length of the trench outside and anxious NCOs began to beat the alarm gongs.

'Come, haul arse!' Red Rudi snarled and ducked as another mortar bomb exploded twenty metres away, showering his helmet with dirt, the shrapnel singing alarmingly through the air, 'get a rope round the shitting nag — and let's get the hell out of here — *quick*!'

Cursing and swearing, the scared men of the firing squad fumbled with the rope, threading it under the stiff body of the dead horse, while below them the noise increased by the instant.

Deltgen, who was guarding the right, cupped his free hand about his mouth and shouted, 'When they come, Rudi, you go with 'em. I'll stay behind a bit and give you fire-support!'

'Christ on a crutch! What's wrong with you? You going nuts or something — volunteering like that!' Rudi broke off suddenly. From down below there came a strange ominous rattle. He flashed a look along the length of the Russian line, now virtually completely shrouded in smoke.

Nothing. But there was no mistaking that squeaky rattle. Another salvo of mortar shells straddled the men toiling up the slope dragging the dead horse after them, faces red with effort. They dropped the rope and fell to the quivering earth. A fist-sized piece of red-hot steel sliced off the dead animal's hind leg and flung it a dozen metres away. Deltgen heard it thwack down onto the snow and raised his head. '*Shit*! The Popovs are carving up our joint before we get it home!' He darted forward as the men rose to their feet and began to drag their burden once more and picked up the frozen leg. With his machine-pistol clutched in one hand and the leg in the other, he backed up the slope, his ears already catching the sounds of the Russians preparing to attack. Any moment now they would burst out of the smoke, pressed shoulder to shoulder, fired-up by the vodka always given to them before an assault, and their political commissars' rousing speeches, crying that blood-chilling 'urrah' of theirs. 'Put some pepper into it,' he cried urgently above the howl of the mortars, 'or we'll never get the bastard back in time! *Heave!*'

Now there was no mistaking the heavy stamp of thousands of boots crunching over the frozen snow below. As usual they were coming in a mass formation. As scared as he was, Deltgen shook his head. The Popovs would never learn, he told himself. Their own machine-gunners would slaughter the poor stupid shits by the hundred. But still, he recalled gloomily, the Popovs seemed to have an inexhaustible supply of cannon fodder.

He flung a glance over his shoulder. The straining, heaving men dragging the horse were nearly there now and behind the rusty hurdles of barbed wire, other men of the 69th were waiting to swing them open and let them through. 'Get on with it!' he cried and with all his strength flung the horse's hindleg towards the anxious waiting riflemen who grabbed it frantically. He swung round again and there they were!

They stamped up the slope, bayonets tucked under their right shoulder, their other arm linked to that of their neighbour, advancing in long grey perfect lines, as if they were back parading on Red Square, their officers and political commissars to the front, crying out orders and exhortations, their breath fogging on the freezing air, their cheeks glowing with good health.

'Holy strawsack!' Deltgen gasped and nearly dropped his Schmeisser with, surprise. 'Would … would you believe it!' Then he recovered. Giving one wild burst which stitched a line of holes in the snow in front of the first rank of marching men, he turned and fled, floundering up the slope as if the devil himself were after him. Down below the Russian infantry burst into song, and thus they advanced to do battle singing lustily, doomed young men all...

The machine-guns hammered away. The Russians fell, row after row of them, blasted to their death by that tremendous wave of lead. Still the ranks behind came marching and singing forward. They seemed so toy like, trivial, ineffective against the metal wrath of the machine-guns sweeping to left and right. To von Dietz watching from the right flank it did not seem that the little grey figures below could be men advancing bravely to certain death. Now, however, the discipline was breaking. The Russians were starting to go to ground. Above the screams, the cries, the curses, the high-pitched hysterical screech of the massed machine-guns, he could hear the throaty chatter of enemy automatic weapons.

Von Dietz snapped out of the awed daze which had overcome him at the sight of those massed singing battalions advancing to be slaughtered like dumb animals. 'Watch that flank!' he cried to the nearest machine-gun nest. 'Swing your weapon round. Friend Ivan'll try to infiltrate! That's his usual trick.'

Unslinging his own machine-pistol, he vaulted over the rusting wire, trying not to see the appalling carnage of writhing, dying Russians everywhere, and crouching low doubled to the edge of the height. He had been right. Other Russians in white camouflaged overalls were winding their way upwards like a huge snake. Whoever the Russian commander was, he had sacrificed a couple of battalions of infantry in order to attempt to surprise the defenders.

Von Dietz brought his m.p. to his right hip and pressed the trigger. It started to chatter at his side. 9mm slugs hissed flatly across the snow. The leading Russians went down and von

Dietz could hear the satisfying thwack-thwack of his bullets striking home. As he crouched there, legs spread, body slightly tensed, spraying the lead from left to right, he told himself he was destroying his fellow human beings. But it never worked. The act of killing gave him a sensation of exhilaration — and he suspected it was the same with all men in battle.

'Bring up that m.g.!' he yelled over his shoulder as more and more white-clad Russians came rushing clumsily out of the fog of war. *'At the double now!'*

The three-man section rose from their pit. With the Spandau cradled in his arms like a baby, the machine-gunner dashed forward, followed by the loader and his number three laden with two hundred pounds of ammunition belts. Lead was now singing its way upwards. The number three came to an abrupt halt, a dazed, bewildered look on his face. Next instant he pitched face-forward onto the churned-up snow. Von Dietz shoved the gunner to the ground. 'Get at it!' he gasped and doubled back to the number three.

He flung him over. He was dead, a neat purple hole, scorched black at the sides, drilled through the centre of his forehead. Von Dietz let him drop again. A ricochet howled off his helmet. He shook his head hard to ward off the blackness which threatened to engulf him. Next moment he picked up the gleaming belts of ammunition and ran back to the gunner sprawled on the ground, bullets stitching a pattern in the snow all around his flying heels. 'Here, for God's sake!' he gasped and thrust the first belt into the waiting hands of the loader.

He fed it in. Next instant the gunner pressed the trigger. At *1,000* rounds a minute, the MG 42 spat fire. Expertly the sweating frantic gunner swung his murderous weapon from side to side. Russians went down everywhere. Still they came on, animated by some desperate wild courage.

Von Dietz raised himself on one knee. He snapped off his empty magazine and rammed home another. He joined in the firing. At his side the loader groaned softly, almost apologetically and keeled over into the snow. Von Dietz continued firing, mentally judging when the sole remaining gunner would need another belt.

The gun chattered to a stop. The Russians gave a wild cry of triumph. They were only fifty metres away now. Von Dietz fired the rest of his magazine at them. He flung the schmeisser down and with frantic fingers that trembled crazily and felt like thick clumsy sausages, he fed another belt of gleaming cartridges into the breech, while at his side the gunner, forgetting all military courtesy and respect in his wild unreasoning fear, cried, 'For fuck's sake — *quick!*'

Just in time, von Dietz threaded it in. The gunner pressed his trigger. Von Dietz prayed there would be no stoppage. The leading Russians were only twenty metres away now. The gun erupted into vicious action. Purple angry flame stabbed the grey air. Screaming obscenely, mad with fear and anger, the gunner swung his gun from left and right, scything his front with death. The yelling Russians seemed to disappear. One minute they were running living men; the next, they were dead or dying, writhing and tossing in the snow, their faces contorted by unbearable agony.

Von Dietz hit the crazed gunner who, still mouthing terrible obscenities, was firing at nothing. 'Cease fire!' he screamed, '*cease-fire, man… They've gone!*'

As if to emphasize that the Russians knew their attack had failed, the first shell of the new barrage burst a hundred metres to their front. A blinding flash, followed by a piercing scream. Von Dietz felt a hot iron sear his shoulder agonizingly. Snow and mud showered down in a fierce rain on his bent helmet.

He blinked open his eyes again. The gunner was holding up his right arm, the blood streaming a bright red down his scorched tattered tunic. A piece of shrapnel had torn off his hand to the wrist. He stared at the bloody ragged gore of the stump, mouthing meaningless little whimpering sounds, as if he could not believe the evidence of his own eyes. 'Come on,' von Dietz croaked, feeling his own arm beginning to go numb. He too had been hit.

Supporting the groaning ashen-faced gunner, whose nose was beginning to acquire that pinched, deathly white look that indicated he was going into fatal shock, von Dietz staggered to their own line.

He dropped to his knees in the first trench. A red mist was threatening to engulf him. Through its wavering confusing tendrils he saw the face gazing up at him from the ground. It was Major Sanders of the First Battalion, his face peaceful, his mouth half-open with his false teeth bulging out from between bloodless lips. His helmet was stoved in into his skull. He was dead, but somehow von Dietz kneeling there next to the dying gunner could not seem to comprehend the fact. 'What the devil is there to laugh about here, Sanders?' he kept saying weakly. 'What indeed?'

It was thus they found him, kneeling next to two dead men, his head bent weakly, as if in defeat...

CHAPTER 3

Colonel von Dietz felt slightly and pleasantly drunk, as he slumped there in the dugout on a ration case, waiting his turn. The Pill had wanted him to take morphia till he could look at his shoulder wound, but von Dietz had refused. If the Russians attacked again this day, he did not want to be unconscious. Instead he had accepted a dozen aspirins and a glass of the Pill's surgical spirit, which had numbed the pain of his wounded shoulder and made him slightly tipsy, so much so that the enormity of what was happening at the far end of the dugout did not seem to affect him as much as it normally did.

The Pill was working flat-out, trying to master the casualties which had piled up during the morning attack. Now they squatted along the sides of the dugout and lay still on stretchers, moaning and whimpering softly to themselves, cursing when the hurrying orderlies stepped on them; while a sweating Pill, his rubber apron red with blood, chopped, sawed and sliced unceasingly, carelessly dropping severed limbs at his feet so that in that hissing flickering light, an observer could have thought he had discovered some horrific human slaughterhouse.

'Excuse me, sir,' a well-known voice cut into von Dietz's reverie.

He turned his head slowly, as if it was worked by stiff springs.

It was Deltgen, a blood-stained bandage wrapped around his head under his helmet.

'I see they gave you a belting too, Deltgen,' von Dietz said, his voice slurred. 'You deserve it as well.'

Deltgen, who had not spoken to the CO since the firing squad incident bit his bottom lip. Behind him the Pill was sawing through another bone, his saw making a high-pitched grating sound that made the small hairs at the back of Deltgen's neck stand on end. 'Yes, sir,' he said in a small voice.

'Well, what is it then?'

'I've got something to report.'

'First of all, did you manage to get that dead nag up here before Friend Ivan paid us a visit? The boys'll need something warm in their guts this day.'

'Yessir. Sarnt-Major Bulle's getting on to it now, sir,' Deltgen said, impatient to make his report, and noticing that the CO with his sleeve tattered and stained with black blood, was slightly drunk. He wondered why.

'All right, make your report, Deltgen.'

'It's me and Rudi, you know —'

'I know who Rudi is, the Berlin rogue,' Colonel von Dietz interrupted him. 'Get on with it.'

'Well, he heard it and I did too, sir. I swear I did and Rudi swears the same. Otherwise I wouldn't have come to see you, especially when you've been...'

Von Dietz smiled softly and a little stupidly. 'What,' he cut in gently, but firmly, 'what did you hear?'

Deltgen gulped hard. Behind him the sawing had ceased and in the gigantic flickering shadow reflected on the wall to his front, he could see the MO tugging at what was left of the shattered leg of the man lying on the table, trying to tear off the remaining skin. He felt he was going to be sick. Hastily he lowered his gaze and whispered thickly, 'Tanks, sir, we heard tanks.'

Von Dietz sat up abruptly, his drunkenness vanished instantly. 'Did you say tanks? But that's impossible. They couldn't get them across the ice on Lake Ladoga, man.' Deltgen gave a stubborn frown. 'I know what I heard, sir. And Rudi too. We're old heads. We wouldn't make a mistake.'

'Perhaps it was a tractor? They'd have had tractors in Leningrad before the siege.'

'No, sir,' Deltgen answered firmly and forced himself to look up. On the wall, the MO was sewing up the man's stump furiously, while at the other table, the sweating hectic orderlies were already preparing the next man for amputation. 'You can always tell a tank. Makes a completely different racket than a tractor. Those big engines of theirs alone are a dead give-away.'

Von Dietz nodded his agreement gloomily, alarming, frightening thoughts beginning to race through his befuddled brain clearing away the fumes of drunkenness rapidly. The 400HP engine used to power the average tank *did* make a hell of a din in comparison with a puny tractor engine!

He rose and guiding a sickened Deltgen by the arm led him out of the groaning misery of the hospital dugout.

Outside the exhausted defenders were mechanically filling magazines with ammunition, cleaning the barrels of their weapons, priming grenades and placing them on the parapets in front of them ready for the next attack. Now, von Dietz told himself, every one of them, young and old, looked a typical 'front swine', hardened infantrymen who had come through hell and would undoubtedly go through hell again and again until its flames finally and inevitably consumed them.

'Now Deltgen, you rogue, where exactly did the sound of this tank — assuming it was one — come from?' von Dietz asked as they stopped near the wire through which the firing-squad party had come.

Cautiously Deltgen peered over the parapet. But there were no snipers out there, just dead men. 'Roughly from the direction of those ruined cottages at ten o'clock, sir,' he said finally. 'But of course, I can't be exactly sure.'

Von Dietz grunted his thanks and focused his glasses on a little settlement of tumble-down, mostly roofless dirty white cottages surrounded by wooden picket fences. There was no sign of life coming from them, but then that didn't surprise him; the Russians were past masters at camouflage and concealment.

Carefully he searched the surface of the snow for the telltale marks of tank tracks, but there were none. The Russians, experts that they were, might well be able to conceal a tank, but the long 75mm cannon of the T-34 was always a give-away; it stuck out half a metre or more in front of the glacis-plate. The gun was always damned difficult to hide. But look as he might, he could not spot it.

He frowned and lowered his glasses for a moment.

'Nothing, sir?' Deltgen asked.

Von Dietz didn't answer. Deltgen *might* have imagined the tank? Yet, he told himself, the little Rhinelander was an experienced soldier who had been with the Regiment since '39; it was unlikely even in the heat of battle that he would let himself be misled. Suddenly he had it. He snapped his fingers together and said, 'Why didn't I think of that before?'

'Think of what, sir?'

Von Dietz had no time to answer. Hurriedly he focused his glasses once again. He swept them around the little settlement, fringing what appeared to be a large straw-roofed barn until finally they came to rest on what he sought: half a dozen tar pots set in the snow, with blackened areas around each one of them, as if at some time or other they had been lit.

'What is it, sir?' Deltgen said excitedly. 'Have you spotted it now, sir?'

Thoughtfully von Dietz lowered his glasses. To their right a burial party under the command of Sergeant-Major Bulle were throwing the dead into a mass grave scratched laboriously in the frozen snow, piling them up on top of each other like so many logs of wood. 'I think it's in that barn — that's the only place where Friend Ivan could hide its gun.'

'How do you know, sir?'

By way of answer, von Dietz handed him the glasses and said, 'Look at those tar pots out there in the snow. What do you think they're there for?'

'*Of course*, sir!' Deltgen, as quick-witted as ever, responded, fiddling with the focus of the binoculars. 'They use them for cold starts.'

'Exactly. In this weather, they'd have to keep the motors going all the time if they didn't want them to freeze over. But the sound would be a give-away. So instead they put the burning tar pots underneath the engine. It's a bit dangerous, but it keeps the engine warm and ready to start at any moment. They've probably got a whole bunch of them going in that barn at this very moment.'

His excitement suddenly forgotten, his face sombre, Deltgen handed the binoculars back to his CO. 'But if they've got tanks, sir, even one of the buggers, how we gonna stop them? Is there even a single sticky grenade in the whole damned Regiment, sir?'

Von Dietz sucked his teeth thoughtfully, feeling the pain in his wounded shoulder begin to throb again. To their right, Bulle was shouting, 'Come on, you cardboard soldiers, let's get these stiffs planted and inside again. This cold's freezing my eggs off'n me!'

Von Dietz frowned. It did not seem the way to treat men who had died bravely for their Regiment and Fatherland, but now they were all becoming brutal. He dismissed Sergeant-Major Bulle and concentrated on the problem at hand.

'I know, Deltgen,' he said finally. 'Of course, we could run away if they put in tanks. But somehow I don't think the Divisional Commander would like that.'

Deltgen laughed hollowly. 'Couldn't Division send up anti-tank weapons, sir?'

'To knock out a T-34, we'd need 57mm anti-tank cannon and they'd never get them and their towing vehicles through the Soviet lines. No, Deltgen, this one we're going to have to manage on our own. The question is — *how*?'

The cold was merciless again. The weary men were starting to give in to it, too tired even to stamp their feet or slap their hands about their hunched skinny shoulders. They simply crouched in their trenches and stared bleakly out at the white, battle-littered Front, roused periodically by NCOs and officers, by shouts and threats, so that they did not commit the fatal mistake of going to sleep. That would have meant frostbite.

Even the red flares sailing into the grey brooding sky above the Russian positions seemed devoid of menace. For the weary frozen infantry they provided nothing more than a source of harmless amusement, a distraction which momentarily took their minds off their misery, and caused a little outburst of conversation.

But all was not mere weariness and resignation in the lines of the 69th Infantry Regiment as that long freezing afternoon began to draw to a close. In the more sheltered dugouts to the rear small groups of old heads were busy, labouring feverishly over the tasks set them by Colonel von Dietz, knowing that speed was of the essence.

Von Dietz had been right that Division would be unable to help them. He had contacted General Degenhardt personally by radio and using the common code, which a cynical von Dietz knew was known to the Russians listening too, he had asked for 'popguns' to help to defend against 'big friends'. The alternative otherwise might be a 'moonlight flit'.

As distorted and vague as the radio link was (for there were hundreds of radio sets now crowded into a small area), he could sense the fat pompous Divisional Commander start at the mention of 'moonlight flit' — the codeword for 'withdrawal'.

'Completely out of the question, Sunflower Three!' he had declared over the crackling radio wave. 'Sunflower One' — he meant Corps HQ — 'could not condone such a move. Over.'

'What about popguns then?' von Dietz had persisted, using the code for anti-tank weapons, imagining as he did so the Soviet radio operators chuckling to themselves as they recognized the word, happy at the German's obvious fear.

'Can't get them through to you, Sunflower Three,' Degenhardt had replied. 'Need 'em ourselves anyway. Sunflower Two' — he meant his own HQ, 'is expecting armour — I mean big friend —' he corrected himself in time, using the code for tanks, 'to attack from across map ref...' he reeled off the grid references, 'at twenty-two hundred this day. Need all the popguns we can get.'

'Then what in three devils' name am I supposed to do, General?' von Dietz had rasped, forgetting wireless procedure in his anger. '*Stick my prick up them?*'

'Von Dietz!' Degenhardt had puffed. 'Please remember procedure and moderate your language, I *am* Sunflower Two after all.'

'Well ... *what?*' von Dietz had insisted grimly.

But there had been no reply. The radio had suddenly gone dead, whether because of Soviet interference or because the General had been unable to find a reply to that overwhelming question, von Dietz had been unable to discover.

It had been then that he had made his decision. While the Pill had dressed his wounded shoulder, probing in the hole for the piece of shrapnel with his instruments, he had explained his plan, what there was of it. 'We'll have to attempt to defend ourselves, Pill,' he had said through gritted teeth, his eyes wet with tears of pain, the sweat trickling down his forehead in thick opaque pearls. 'We've got your surgical spirit and the last of the gasoline used for delousing.'

'Molotov cocktails?' the Pill had queried, digging his probe a little deeper into the gleaming red flesh, miserable at the pain he was causing his friend by doing so.

'Yes.'

'But that wouldn't be enough — and by God, the men who'll throw them will have to be damned brave, you know yourself.'

Von Dietz nodded, feeling the hot salty taste of blood in his mouth where he had bitten through his bottom lip in his agony. 'We'll have tied charges too,' he grunted.

The Pill knew what he meant: several grenades strapped together to provide a more powerful explosion that sometimes was effective underneath a tank if a man could succeed in getting the primitive mine in place there. '*And that's all?*' he asked, finally succeeding in extracting the gleaming silver piece of metal and dropping the shrapnel into the blood-filled dish.

'That's all,' von Dietz echoed weakly, letting his head slump for a moment, while the Pill set about staunching the new flow of blood.

'My God, if that's all you've got, Horst, we'd better start praying — *now!*'

With the last of his strength, von Dietz raised his head. 'I've heard of worse ideas, Pill,' he said.

So now they waited, as the long black shadows raced across the snow and the red signal flares tinged the sky a blood-red hue. It wouldn't be long now…

CHAPTER 4

The huge shell tore the night silence apart terrifyingly. With a hellish crash it exploded a hundred metres beneath the defence line. Flame spurted high. A great fountain of blossoming earth followed. The defenders crouched low as it came down again, raining pebbles and soil onto their bent helmets. 'Here we go,' Deltgen cried above the roar, 'the band concert has started! They're tuning up —'

He didn't finish. Another great shell howled from the Russian positions and slammed into the earth a hundred metres behind them, making the very ground tremble and shimmy beneath their feet, sucking the air from their lungs so that they fought and gasped for breath.

'Ranging in!' Red Rudi screamed, pressing his mouth close to Deltgen's ear, so that he could be heard.

And then the tremendous bombardment swamped their positions as the Russian fire softened them up yet once again for what was soon to come. The night became a screaming, red-roaring nightmare. Shrapnel hissed everywhere. Men fell screaming piteously. A shellshocked soldier threw away his rifle and broke from the cover of the trench. He didn't get five metres, a shell ripped him to shreds the next instant.

How long that barrage lasted, no one ever knew later. For some it seemed a matter of moments, for others years. Then as abruptly as it had started it ended, leaving behind a loud echoing tense silence.

The officers and noncoms reacted immediately. Those who were still alive dragged themselves out of the earth steaming debris which covered them, amazed as they did so at this transformed world around them and started to blow shrill blasts on their whistles. '*Stand to! ... stand to!*' the cry went from foxhole to foxhole. For now the Soviet flares filled the sky everywhere to their front; and among the green for artillery support and the red of the infantry, there was a new colour erupting in the darkness which chilled the old heads to the bone. '*Violet!*' they croaked to the bewildered scared greenbeaks who had never seen that particular flare before. 'Violet ... that means ... *tank support!*'

The Pill, his wounded tended for the time being, burst out of the hospital bunker followed by his orderlies and kicked open the tin door of the dugout which housed the kitchen bulls and Sergeant-Major Bulle, their faces yellow with fear by the light of the wildly flickering candles. 'Everyone out and into the line! ... CO's orders... We need every rifle possible this night... *COME ON NOW. FRIEND IVAN IS PUTTING IN TANKS!*'

'*Tanks!*' The Bull quavered and blind with fear reeled to the exit.

'There they are, sir!' Deltgen cried excitedly, pointing to the left flank. 'Next to that bunch of shattered trees, sir. Can you see?'

Von Dietz swung his head in the direction indicated, his ears still ringing with the infernal din of that terrible barrage.

Yes, there they were. Three squat T-34s emerging out of the smoke, spread out over a front of perhaps a hundred metres, and behind each armoured monster, its gun moving to left and right in search of its prey, a phalanx of tense crouched infantry, armed with bayonets.

'If we could only have dug in deeper,' somebody behind the watching officer groaned. 'Now they'll squash us flat in these shallow pits!'

'Oh, go and shit in yer helmet!' Red Rudi snarled angrily. 'Stop moaning — you'll have me pissing down my leg in half a minute, arse with ears!'

Von Dietz's mind raced, as the forty-ton monsters crawled ever closer to their position, the tracer bouncing off their sides like ping-pong balls. Their appearance had apparently paralysed most of the defenders, they were making no attempt to tackle the infantry coming up behind the cover of the tanks.

The Russians had made their usual mistake of lifting the barrage too early. That gave the defenders the chance to raise their heads and react. But how? First they would have to get rid of the accompanying infantry, outlined a stark black against the flares which cast their lurid eerie light on the scene below.

'All right, you heroes!' he cried, breaking that awed silence at last. 'Let's get their infantry first. From the flank, you cardboard soldiers!'

Standing there completely exposed on the parapet, knowing as he did so that he was being foolishly reckless, he wrenched back the trigger cock of his machine-pistol and sprayed a burst of 9mm bullets at the mass of metal and man moving towards the 69th.

That burst of fire roused the men from their terrified stupor, that inactive waiting for destruction under the roaring whirring tracks of the T-34s. As one they poured a hail of slugs at the Russians crouching behind the tanks. Suddenly the surprised infantry were galvanized into violent frenetic action, swinging round crazily, throwing up their arms, crumpling with vicious fury, turning their ranks in bloody chaotic confusion.

The gunners in the T-34s were inexperienced, a grateful von Dietz realized, as the tanks clattered on, leaving behind them a carpet of dead and dying soldiers, with here and there a crazed man trying to keep up with the monsters, running and shouting hopelessly until he, too, was mowed down by that cruel fire. Instead of turning their machine-guns on the men standing clearly exposed on the parapets, they opened up with their cannon.

'Like trying to swat a shitting fly with a shitting hammer!' Deltgen roared scornfully, as with a tremendous whoosh the first hundred-pound shell ripped the air apart above their heads and exploded in a great black mushroom of smoke and flying earth to their rear. Those Popovs must have their brains in their arses!'

'Thank God, they have!' von Dietz cried back. 'Come on you, heroes, let's go and get them, now they've lost their escorts!'

Crouched low, laden with their burdens, the little group of men that von Dietz had prepared specially for this mission swung open the wire hurdles and crept into no-man's land, all of them knowing that the likelihood of their coming out alive in this unequal contest between man and monster was very small.

Swiftly they approached the tanks, dodging from hole to hole, throwing themselves flat in the churned-up snow every time a flare exploded overhead colouring the ground blood-red and glowing green before raising themselves and darting on once more.

Now they were only fifty metres away from the T-34s still blazing away with HE rounds at the positions above. The noise was deafening. Every time the 75mms fired, they felt the hot blast and sensed their uniforms whipped about their lean bodies by the wave of explosive. Still the Russians hadn't spotted them. Now Colonel von Dietz, working his way to the left flank of the leading T-34, began to think they might get away with this suicidal attack after all. Perhaps the Russians weren't as invincible as they thought they were, hidden inside their steel boxes.

He dropped into a foxhole. Deltgen and Red Rudi, both armed with satchel charges, did the same sprawling onto the ground behind him, feeling it tremble and rumble under the weight of the advancing monster. 'See that shell-hole to the left,' he gasped. 'Into that and let the thing roll over us. Then we'll tackle it from the rear!'

He heard Deltgen give an audible gulp and he knew why. The prospect of letting that forty-ton tank roll over one frightened even the bravest of men. One slip and those racing tracks would churn the unlucky man to a bloody pulp. 'I'll recommend you for the close-combat badge, if we pull it off,' he cried above the roar of the tank's labouring engine. It was a weak joke, for they had earned that decoration long ago.

'To hell with that, sir!' Rudi snarled. 'Recommend me for a nice safe job in an old soldiers' home instead!'

'You wouldn't last the week,' von Dietz called. 'Come on — *LOS!*'

The three of them rose as one. With a desperate burst of energy they pelted forward and caught a last glimpse of the monster towering above them, blocking out everything as they dived into the steaming shell-hole.

There they lay, hearts pounding furiously, nerves electric with overwhelming fear as the roar of those deadly tracks got closer and closer, its clanking and rattling drowning every other sound.

'*Duck!*' von Dietz screamed.

They bent their heads. The monster was above them. The din was tremendous. Their ears threatened to burst at any moment. Their nostrils were full of the cloying nauseating stink of oil. They cowered, feeling hot oil drip on their backs, as the churning tracks, only centimetres away from their frail huddled bodies, began to cross the pit. Their world was a black, howling pit. It seemed never ending. Von Dietz felt the air sucked cruelly from his lungs. He started to gasp. He was choking. He couldn't stand it any longer. He'd throw himself under the nearest track. Let the steel monster have its way with him. Only let it end...

And then it was gone and they were breathing in the stench of diesel mixed with cold night air. To their rear, the T-34's exhaust glowed a dull-red in the darkness. *They'd done it!*

Groggily, von Dietz rose to his feet. 'Come on,' he croaked weakly, 'come on before it gets too far...'

Like sleep-walkers they stumbled through the churned-up mud after the roaring monster, which rolled on so triumphantly unaware of this latter-day David out to slaughter it.

Now they were only five metres away. They could feel the tremendous heat engendered by the twin exhaust. 'Watch it!' von Dietz warned above the ear-splitting roar. 'Don't grab the exhausts. They'd burn your flesh off to the bone. *NOW!*'

Reaching for the towing hook, he pulled himself up and on to the tank. Next moment Deltgen and Red Rudi did the same.

'Where, sir?' Deltgen cried, holding up the satchel charge. Von Dietz's brain raced. Even the multiple grenades would have little impact on the steel hide of this forty-ton Goliath. He had to pick its weak spot. 'The turret,' he cried. 'We'll try to knock out the turret ring... Then a parcel over the side onto the right track.'

They clambered upwards.

Inside someone must have heard the clatter of their steel-shod boots on the tank's deck.

'*Duck!*' von Dietz screamed frantically, as suddenly there was the soft whirr of electricity and the gun came swinging round in an attempt to swat them off.

It missed them by millimetres as they crouched there, whipping its heated barrel so close that they could feel the warmth through their tunics. They didn't give it a second chance at trying to swat them off. Hastily with trembling fingers they packed two of the satchels close to the joint between the turret and deck and pulled the strings. 'Over the side!' von Dietz screamed above the sudden chatter of the turret machine-gun, as the unknown Russian gunners made a second attempt to get rid of them. Flinging his own packed grenades into racing bogies, he dived over the side, rolled over, just evading the stream of white tracer which cut the air above him and fell into a shell-hole.

There was a thick muffled crump of explosive. Another followed immediately. The right track snapped abruptly and rolled behind the tank like a severed link. The turret heaved. Puffs of smoke-came pouring out of the metal seams. Someone screamed. Next instant the hatch was thrown open. A man appeared, eyes wild with terror, his uniform already rent by flame. Von Dietz did not give him a chance. He aimed from the hip as he lay there. The burning Russian flailed the air crazily with his hands. Next moment he flopped over the edge of the turret, dead, the flames leaping up greedily to consume him.

The second tank went up in flame, as the men took suicidal risks to fling their Molotov cocktails, here and there being mown down by the T-34's chattering machine-guns, turning it into a hellish steel cauldron which bubbled with fire and destruction.

It was all too much for the driver of the third T-34. He swung his vehicle round, showering the men waiting to destroy it with soil and pebbles, and in a roar of clashing gears, sent it scurrying for safety down the slope, followed by the cheers of the defenders.

Von Dietz stared dazed after it, bewildered by its disappearance, or so it seemed. After the nervous tension of the last few hours, he felt suddenly confused, perhaps even slightly mad, as if he had just won a great lottery — the lottery of life-and-death.

Then slowly it began to dawn on him. They had done it! They were saved. For the time being they had been reborn. They had beaten the tanks!

Deltgen, his face black, dirty smudges on his bandaged bare head, appeared. He grinned at von Dietz standing there, his teeth very white against the black, his hair glowing in the light of the flares. 'Sir —' he started.

Von Dietz did not give him a chance to finish his sentence. He clasped him into his arms, laughing till tears started to run down his worn exhausted face, slapping his sides and shoulders uproariously, crying over and over again, as if he would never stop, *'We've beaten them … we've beaten them, do you hear … beaten…'*

To the east over Leningrad the sky started to lighten — reluctantly, as if God himself was hesitant to throw light on the war-torn, crazy world below; and in that 18th century bunker, the two men sat staring at each other, smoking in silence as the old clock on the wall ticked away the minutes of life with metallic inexorability, wondering…

CHAPTER 5

It was a sound unlike any the battered defenders of the Height had ever heard before. As the sun slid over the lip of the horizon the day after they had beaten off the tank attack, there was a dull groaning noise. Once! Twice! A hard-pink flash stabbed the darkening sky. They stared at the sudden light in wonder, rubbing their unshaven chins with doubt. A low roar which became a high-pitched baleful scream, and rose to a furious, elemental howl, blotting out all else; and then the fiery-red missiles which came screeching across the sky straight to plunge down and burst with antiphonal impact, scattered dismembered bodies on all sides, drenching the survivors in the blood of the slaughtered. The bombardment of the Pimple with Soviet Russia's latest weapon, which Zhdanov had personally requested from Stalin, had commenced. The *katuskas* — or 'Stalin's organs', as the stubble-hoppers would one day learn to call them — had made their appearance on the Leningrad Front!

All that night and well into the following morning, the Pimple was subjected to their terrible fire, while the defenders quaked and cowered in their holes in abject misery as the earth reared and bucked like a wild horse put to the saddle for the first time around them. The fearsome rockets swamped everything, keeping up their pressure until their shelling had merged into one continuous cyclonic roar.

It was as if some great angry giant was shaking the very earth, as rocket after rocket plunged down out of the burning sky curving towards the trench line — or what was left of it — in a glowing parabola to explode like a volcano, spewing forth fire.

On and on the barrage went. Men went mad. Others killed themselves. A few relapsed into blessed unconsciousness, unaware that they were soaked in their own waste products. But for the rest, caught in the heart of that seething cauldron of terrible fire, it had to be endured; their miserable little bodies huddled together, tightly clenched fists pressed into their ears, mouths wide open and gasping against the tremendous blast, eyes wide and wild with overwhelming fear.

This time, as the red signal flares burst into the sky indicating that the enemy was going to attack again, the bombardment did not cease. Instead the massed ranks of Russian infantry advanced behind a wave of rolling mortar fire, plodding behind it thoughtfully, even sadly like farmers returning home tired and weary after a long day's toil in the fields, stunned by the thunder of the guns as they trudged up that bitter slope.

Now the mortar barrage added its fury to that of the rockets as it descended upon the hilltop positions, the pillars of smoke caused by the exploding shells rising swiftly to the black-bellied clouds.

Still the survivors did not move. They couldn't. That tremendous bombardment pinned them to their holes, as the shrapnel clattered from their helmets and the earth below reeled and smashed them in their cramped bodies every time another of the fearsome rockets slammed down. They were absorbed by a fear against which there was no weapon: the fear of this depersonalized, machine-made death.

Now the solid ranks of the Russians began to break up into groups, as they entered the smoking, shell-holed, cratered confusion of the German first line. Numbly, like dumb animals, the survivors crouching there allowed themselves to be slaughtered where they crouched, seemingly not feeling the sharp bayonets stabbed into their backs or the crash of brass-bound rifle butts which shattered their bent skulls.

Then suddenly the barrage stopped. It was dangerous in that confusion for the Soviet gunners to continue firing; they might hit their own men.

In the second line the survivors started to rouse themselves. Like men waking from some long drawn out nightmare, they raised their weary heads, eyes wild and wide with shock, to view the transformed landscape in front of them, now swarming with enemy soldiers, emerging from the smoke like grey ghosts.

Von Dietz stared uncomprehendingly for a long moment. His eardrums continued to thunder agonizingly by themselves. He blinked his eyes several times, seeing the vague shapes through the brown mist of acrid fumes and smoke, yet somehow not able to identify them. For a while his gaze fixed itself on a severed leg, complete with boot, as if the bloody stump was of importance. To his right, one of their own machine-guns chattered hysterically for a few moments and Russians stumbled, clutched their bodies and tumbled to the ground before the m.g. disappeared in the scarlet flash of an exploding grenade.

But the sudden sharp noise roused him from his dreamlike bemused state at last. Suddenly he was burningly conscious of the desperate state of the Regiment and its position. He flung wild glances to left and right. His dead lay everywhere. But there were men alive. He could see them crouching in their foxholes, passively awaiting the Russians, as numb and petrified as he had just been. With frantic fingers, he tugged out his officer's whistle and blew a shrill blast on it to attract their attention. Slowly, as if their heads were activated by stiff rusty springs, they turned their gaze in his direction. In a frenzy of gesturing, he indicated what they should do, as the Russians came nearer and nearer.

They understood. They let their heads sink and weapons fall, but within easy reach of their hands, as they feigned death. Now the first wave of cautious Russians, bodies half-crouched, rifles tucked suspiciously into their sides, started to move through the apparent dead, eyes searching the fog of war to their front for the German enemy. A soldier stepped on von Dietz's hand and he bit back his yelp of agony just in time. The first wave passed.

Cautiously von Dietz raised his head. The second wave was still not yet in sight. They'd be perhaps another hundred metres off. It was time to go. He sprang to his feet. Standing there on the lip of his shattered foxhole, he blew a shrill blast on his whistle and raised his machine-pistol. '*Los*!' he cried. '*At the dogs, soldiers*!' His men needed no urging. They had suffered enough. Now they were going to take their revenge.

Like a pack of wild animals they surged forward after von Dietz. Screaming in wild triumph, they slammed into the rear of the Russian first wave. The Russians turned, their eyes full of horror, as these grey, ragged, crazed men flung themselves at them. Too late!

In a flash the stubble-hoppers of the 69th were in among them. Bayonets flashed. Entrenching tools came cleaving down on shaven Russian skulls. Slipping in the snow and churned up earth, the soldiers reeled back and forth, carried away by a blood-hot elemental fury. But there was no stopping the wild men of the shattered infantry regiment. Russian after Russian went down to be hacked to death on the ground and then suddenly they were through and racing for the safety of the last trench. The path they took was carpeted with the mutilated bodies of Russian soldiers.

The silence hung like a bad nightmare over the shattered ground. Here and there a wounded survivor continued to limp slowly towards the third and last line of defence under the icy-cold silver light of the stars.

Wearily the defenders — what was left of them — stared at the late arrivals. No one moved to help them. What was the use? Tomorrow they'd all be dead anyway. Now all of them were tormented by the overwhelming realization that they were living without hope. That the morrow would be the same as today, only worse. Scarcely a man spoke. When they did, all they had to say was a few choked, meaningless phrases which more often than not trailed away into nothing, as if it were not worth speaking anymore. Speech called for just too much effort.

Von Dietz slumped next to the Pill, who was doing his best to treat a soldier whose intestines were hanging out, but who was too far gone even to groan. In these last four years of war he and the Regiment had been in many desperate situations. But never in all those years had he felt such an overwhelming sense of utter ruin as he did now. More than once the Regiment had been decimated and he had still been confident that it could survive. But now... He let his gloomy thoughts have full rein, while the wounded soldier died silently under the Pill's hands.

With a sigh the old doctor straightened up and wiped his blood-soaked hands on his ragged trousers before reaching out and closing the dead man's eyelids; then as an afterthought, he pulled the cape off a dead man next to him and covered the obscene hole in the corpse's stomach with it.

'Well, Horst?' he asked in a hoarse dry voice.

It seemed to take the younger man a long time to register. Finally he said, 'I don't know, Pill ... I frankly don't know.' He looked at his filthy bloody hands miserably.

'You could close down the shop?' the Pill said softly.

Von Dietz shook his head. 'There'll be no surrender to Friend Ivan. They are not bad people basically. But after what we have done to them and the way they have been treated by their own masters since the Revolution...' He shrugged and concluded lamely: 'I haven't much faith in our ability to survive in a Russian POW Camp, Pill.'

The night passed slowly. The miserable remnant of the 69th Regiment huddled on the ridge, most of them fast asleep, careless of normal military precautions. They were too exhausted and resigned to their fate to care any longer, and the surviving officers made little attempt to rouse their men. They too had lost all hope. The morrow meant death or captivity, which was the same thing in the long run. What did anything matter?

Dawn came reluctantly. The first grey light intensified the worn pallor of the exhausted men. They roused themselves with difficulty. Mechanically they went about the pre-dawn routine; urinating in hot yellow streams against the walls of their trenches; rubbing snow on their dirty faces; cleaning frost from the barrels of their weapons; pulling back the bolts a few times to check that they had not frozen up; some smoking the last of their cigarettes, and the lucky ones munching on a last crust of bread. Then they slumped there and waited. For the end.

But that was not to be this day. At approximately eight that morning as the Russians dug in in the ruined trenches only a hundred metres away from the ridge started to fire off the usual red flares indicating that a new infantry attack would soon be launched, though this time without artillery support because of the danger to their own men, a small man stumbled into the 69th's lines. He escaped being shot because the soldier on guard was too weary and too slow. By the time he had reacted the small man was inside the trench with him and speaking German quickly.

Five minutes later he was introducing himself to a bewildered Pill and von Dietz with a kind of formality they had forgotten existed, 'Krause, Captain, staff, gentlemen.'

The two of them stared at the officer who was puny like a boy, his cheeks so sunken that they looked as if he deliberately sucked them in.

'Did you say … *staff*?' von Dietz croaked.

'Yessir,' the small man said and taking out a gold cigarette case offered the other two officers a real cigarette, as if he did not know that he was tendering an infinitely precious gift. 'General Degenhardt sent me personally — and I must say it was damnably difficult getting up here. Those Popov chaps are everywhere, aren't they?'

The two of them nodded their heads like village idiots, not wanting to waste one precious bit of the beautiful soothing smoke the weed afforded.

'Had to shoot one of them,' he continued in his bright manner. 'First chap I've shot in four years of war. Surprising, isn't it, when you come to think of it, gentlemen?'

Again they nodded mutely, taking in his features greedily, tracing the course of his nose, his chin, the way he was cleanly shaven, with just a suspicion of real soap in the left eardrum, absorbing the good clean smell that came from him, noting the clear white of his eyes, and the way his teeth gleamed as if they might well be brushed three times a day with genuine toothpaste.

He did not seem to notice this strange intense scrutiny, as he rattled on about his adventures between lines on his way up to the ridge. 'Quite good fun in a way, gentlemen, though of course nothing to be compared with staff work back at Div. I mean there one does have a great deal of responsibility. Can't afford to relax for one minute, whereas here, one can really let go, clean out the system in a way, as one might say…' He stopped suddenly as the two of them numbly held out their hands again. 'Another smoke, gentlemen?' he queried.

They nodded in unison.

'Not good for you, the old lung-torpedoes, they say,' he said heartily and offered them his case again. 'At least that's what they say, don't they?'

Greedily they snatched another precious cigarette from the case and lit them from the glowing stump, sucking in great gulps of smoke.

'Well, I suppose you are wondering why I am here,' Krause continued. 'I shall tell you. The situation on the Leningrad Front has changed drastically. While the Popovs have been attacking all this last week, our chaps at the rear have been building a new defensive line skirting the Narva River and between the banks of Lakes Chudskoye and Pskovskoye, code-named Panther.'

He beamed at the two ragged scarecrows winningly. 'Division has now been ordered to pull back to it… Well, as a consequence, Degenhardt, excuse me, we on the staff do get a little careless of titles and ranks — familiarity breeds, well, *General* Degenhardt I mean, has requested me to tell you that you must withdraw.'

'*Withdraw?*' von Dietz croaked. 'Did you say — *withdraw?*'

'Yessir,' he answered brightly. 'As soon as it is convenient. The plan is this. *Luftwaffe-One* has been alerted. They are going to provide a squadron of Stukas. As soon as you are ready, they will...' Captain Krause broke off suddenly and stared at the Pill in awed wonder. Gentle tears were beginning to trickle slowly down his worn, lined face...

CHAPTER 6

Over Leningrad the sky flushed pink time and time again. It was the colour of the permanent barrage. But von Dietz and the other watching officers concealed at the edge of the ridge had no eyes for the barrage. They were searching for something else.

Closer at hand, there were occasional bursts of machine-gun fire from the Russians dug in metres away, as if they were very nervous and expected some final desperate suicidal charge from the Germans trapped on the ridge. Here and there there was the flash of bright glass, as an officer watched the German line through his binoculars for the first sign of movement.

'Friend Ivan is damned confident,' von Dietz said a little bitterly.

'How do you mean, Colonel?' Krause asked, obviously enjoying his 'little jaunt to the front', as he called it.

'Those people over there watching us. They aren't taking the most elementary precautions against our snipers. Obviously they think we're virtually beat.'

'And they wouldn't be too far wrong,' the Pill growled, indicating the nearest soldier, his head nodding and falling constantly as he tried desperately to fight off sleep.

Von Dietz nodded. 'I know. But with a bit of luck, he'll be sleeping the clock round soon — all of us will.' He tapped the timber to his front three times for luck.

'Don't worry, sir,' Krause said cheerfully. 'The fly-boys will be on time. The General has promised the squadron ten cases of pink Crimean champus if they pull this one off.'

'Crimean champagne against men's lives,' the Pill said and shook his greying head. 'What a funny world!'

'The best of all possible worlds,' Krause commenced and stopped suddenly.

'What is it?' the Pill asked sharply.

'There they are,' Krause said excitedly, 'right on time! Very good, eh?'

Dietz did not reply. Instead he focused his glasses in the direction in which Krause was pointing. He was right. There they were — nine stark-black shapes set against the pink glow over Leningrad. Hastily he adjusted the binoculars. The typical unmistakable gull-like shapes of the Stuka dive bomber leapt into the gleaming circle of glass. He let the glasses fall to his chest and cried, 'Sarnt-Major Bulle!'

'Sir?'

'Sound the stand-to... *They're here!*'

Krause leapt excitedly. 'Oh, I say,' he chortled with delight. 'Now for the fun and games!'

'Fun and games indeed,' the Pill echoed grimly, as the Stukas, which had made a wide circle from the west out into the Gulf of Finland in order not to be spotted on the ground, came winging in landwards, taking the anti-aircraft defences by complete surprise.

At 300 kilometres an hour they came racing in through the puffballs of brown smoke in their typical wedge-shaped formation.

Boom ... boom ... boom, the flak thundered. Twice von Dietz could have sworn one of the gull-winged planes had been struck, but each time it came rushing through the smoke unharmed.

Then they were directly above the hilltop positions. The Pill swallowed apprehensively. 'I hope those fly-boys know their job,' he said. 'It would be sheer slaught —'

'They'll see the identification panels we've put out,' Krause reassured him. 'They're very expert. They've dive-bombed their way across half of Europe —' He stopped short and watched as the formation hovered directly above them, their wheels extended like the searching talons of birds-of-prey selecting their victims.

The leading plane waggled its wings.

'Here they come!' Krause yelled.

With an unearthly, spine-chilling scream the first plane flung itself out of the shell-pocked sky. Going full-out, its sirens screaming frenetically, it hurtled towards the earth. On and on. Down and down. Nothing seemed able to prevent it smashing itself to a myriad pieces on the ground. Von Dietz caught his breath, his clenched fists wet with sweat. The pilot could never pull the dive-bomber out of that death-defying dive!

But at the very last moment, he did. The plane seemed to stagger in mid-air. A host of tiny black eggs came tumbling in crazy profusion from its evil blue-painted belly.

'*Bombs*!' Krause screamed carried away by a wild excitement as the first plane began to climb and the next one dropping out of the sky came hurtling down in an ear-splitting dive.

Bomb explosions rippled the length of the trench opposite them. Abruptly it bubbled with fire and destruction. Palls of black smoke mushroomed upwards immediately, and through it the plane came hurtling down at four hundred kilometres an hour, sirens going full-out.

Now the weary veterans started to clamber out of their holes, staring, bewildered, at the thickening clouds of smoke rising to their front, ignoring the howl of shrapnel which cut the air from the Soviet positions. They smiled at each other. Here a man slapped a comrade across the shoulders, as if in triumph, while others gawped open-mouthed like idiots. A couple sprang up and down in delight. One sobbing youth raised his head and cried across at von Dietz, in a tear-filled voice, 'We're saved, Colonel! We're saved... Oh, my God ... *saved*!'

'Give the shits a bellyful!' the voices rose on all sides, as plane after plane came hurtling down to discharge their cargoes of death. 'Knock the crap out of 'em!... Make them suffer too... That'll show the red bastards...'

Von Dietz's face hardened again. Now he was businesslike, his momentary euphoria at this impossible stroke of luck and change of fortune forgotten. There was no time to waste. They had to make the most of it. 'Form up ... *form up*!' he bellowed above the scream of the Stukas' sirens. 'Sections, get ready to move out!... *At the double now*!'

'*At the double now*!' the cries went up on all sides, as the men, suddenly animated by new energy, rushed to take their places in their sections. They were going to evacuate the damned Pimple; there was no time to be wasted.

Von Dietz fired his last flare. It exploded above the height with a soft plop, colouring their upturned faces an eerie, glowing, unnatural green. Without any further ado, von Dietz pumped his right arm up and down three times. At his side Krause said, 'I say, here we go again!' Next to him, the Pill spat drily into the dirty snow.

A slow Soviet m.g. started to chatter. Tracer bullets zipped through the air towards them as they stumbled down the battle-littered slope westwards. A shell exploded metres away and flooded the greyness with a blood-red light. Von Dietz broke into an awkward weary run. They did the same. '69th, *follow me*!' he cried in a broken voice.

'*At them, lads!*' Krause exclaimed, snapping off excited shots to left and right with his pistols.

Russians were springing up out of their trenches on all sides. But there was no stopping these wild ragged men who had appeared so suddenly out of nowhere. In an instant they had turned the defenders' line into confused chaos. A Russian attempted to bar von Dietz's progress. Krause shot him in the stomach before he could throw his grenade. He went down clasping it to his stomach. It exploded a moment later, ripping his body to shreds, showering the men running by it in great gouts of blood. A man with a long old-style bayonet ran at von Dietz. He slapped the barrel of his m.p. down hard on the hands holding the weapon. The Russian yelped with unbearable pain and let the bayonet fall. Next instant, von Dietz's boot had slammed into his face. The features disappeared in a mess of red gore.

The fight went out of the Russians. One moment they were fighting desperately to stop this sudden attack; the next they were broken, clutching and clawing at each other in their frenzied attempt to escape from these barbaric creatures in grey, throwing away their weapons, streaming down the hillside screaming with fear, as if the devil himself were after them.

Leather-lunged and gasping hectically, the survivors of the 69th Regiment of Infantry followed, and behind them emerging from the grey fog of war like some great ghastly ghost stood Height 560 — 'the Pimple', abandoned for good, littered with the bodies of nearly a thousand young men — old heads and greenbeaks — who had wasted their lives for it. But as the survivors limped towards their own lines, where their rescuers, overcome by wonder at the sight of these ragged skeletons advancing upon them, were starting to cheer, they did not look back. The Pimple was already history...

'Watch it!' the Bull growled.

The survivors shambled into some form of readiness, as the General's staff car came slowly into the farmyard, its general officer's flag flying proudly at the grey bonnet. They were utterly exhausted now, some without boots, others with new bandages around old wounds, all dirty, starving, lice-ridden and at the end of their tether.

'Look at 'em,' Red Rudi grumbled to Deltgen who was swaying with weariness next to him, hardly able to keep his eyes open, 'crawling out of their gold-plated bunkers to have a look at the wild front swine.' He spat contemptuously as General Degenhardt, followed by his elegant chief-of-staff and a be-monocled adjutant, stepped from the Mercedes.

With the last of his strength, Colonel von Dietz, the left leg of his trousers ripped off to reveal a white calf flecked with drying black blood, limped forward and saluted. '69th Regiment of Infantry, fourteen officers, forty NCOs and one thousand five hundred other ranks — present and correct, *sir!*' he reported in the regulation fashion.

General Degenhardt's fleshy, crimson face registered his shock all too clearly and behind him the adjutant's monocle popped out of his right eye with surprise. The casualty rate was tremendous; it meant the 69th had left half its strength on Height 560.

'Good-day, von Dietz,' Degenhardt stuttered, attempting to recover his composure for general officers were supposed never to show shock. 'Good to see you... But did you say fifteen hundred?'

'I did, sir,' von Dietz answered stonily, swaying slightly.

'That's fifty per cent casualties,' the Chief-of-Staff grunted.

'Intolerable, General. Can't take casualties like that much longer.'

Later von Dietz would recall that 'much longer', but now he was too weary to react. 'Permission to stand the men at ease, sir?' he requested.

'Of course, of course, my dear fellow. I'm sure they must be rather … tired,' he beamed, fat face full of fake bonhomie.

Von Dietz creaked round awkwardly. '69th Regiment,' he called, '69th Regiment, stand at — *ease!*'

If the General had expected the harsh, well-ordered crash of fifteen hundred boots stamping down on the snow, he was disappointed; all he got was a weary shuffle. Still he continued to smile hugely, as if he did not see that strange blank expressionless look in their eyes like that of a dead animal and their faces hollowed out like grey death's heads.

'Soldiers,' he barked in his best pre-war parade ground voice, 'I should like to express my thanks — and the thanks of our Fatherland, Folk and Führer for what you have done. Er, we at Division are proud of you.' He paused and looked round their faces, as if he half-expected to see a glow of pride and joy at his words. But there was none.

'Your sacrifice has been great, very great indeed. But let me tell you,' he raised his voice emotionally, 'it has not been in vain. It has given our army the time it needed to regroup. Now we are in such a strong position that nothing, I repeat, *nothing*, that the red barbarians can send against us will be able to break through.' His face radiated belief, absolute, one hundred per cent conviction that he was right. 'Now you will have a period of rest and refitment before you too take your place in that impregnable line. Soldiers of the 69th Infantry Regiment,' General Degenhardt snapped to attention and raised his hand to the gleaming peak of his cap, standing very erect, tense and emotional (later von Dietz would recall that there were real tears coursing down his fat well-fed face), '*I, your General, salute you!*'

Wearily the ragged survivors began to file past him on their way to the rear, while he stood there rigidly to attention. Von Dietz gave him a half-hearted salute, then he trailed after his men. The General, he told himself, wasn't a bad little man really. He believed intensely in his army; there weren't many left like him in 1943...

BOOK THREE: *THE WAY BACK*

'He was a different man. Something had come to him, which had not yet come to us. It was the trial of battle and no one who passes through it is ever quite the same again.'

H. Allen.

CHAPTER 1

Colonel von Dietz came out of the hectic hustle of Berlin's Lehrter Station where the troop trains steaming in from the Front at one minute intervals were being greeted by crying, hysterical, happy crowds of women and children, waving the small swastika paper flags handed to them by the Hitler Youth. Von Dietz, leaning on his cane, stared a little bewildered at the emotional scene in front of him.

Berlin seemed shabbier than ever. Undernourished men and women, their heads ducked in the collars of their shabby coats, hurried on between the still smoking ruins of last night's RAF bombing raid, while ancient wood-burning taxis and trucks trundled down the bomb-littered streets, their open backs packed with earnest-looking businessmen with their briefcases at the ready. And everywhere there were the wounded in their striped hospital uniforms, hobbling about on their crutches, or the blind, with the dotted armbands on their sleeves, tapping their way with newly acquired hesitation between the ruins. His gaze fell on the large white banner suspended from the office building opposite, 'WE THANK THEE, O, OUR FÜHRER!' the black inscription proclaimed proudly.

An old woman in ill-fitting men's trousers carefully gathering up the cigarette-ends tossed away in the gutter by the departing soldiers saw the look on the young Colonel's face as he read the message and winked knowingly. 'Thank him, we can, sir, can't we?' she said in a thick Berlin accent. 'Without him we would never have had this.' Again she winked cheekily.

Von Dietz winked back. At least the Berliners were remaining sane. 'That you can say again, Granny,' he said and began to limp down the street on his cane.

It had been the Pill's idea that he should report sick to the divisional surgeon and obtain specialist treatment at Berlin's famed *la charité* hospital. 'It's no use fooling yourself, Horst,' he had stated severely, after examining the younger man's leg carefully at the little Russian seaside resort where what was left of the 69th had been withdrawn to rest and refit as General Degenhardt had promised. 'Without specialist treatment that leg of yours is going to give you trouble for the rest of your days.'

He had laughed and said, 'How many do you seriously think they will be, you old fool?… With the wastage rate of infantry officers being what it is.'

'All right,' the Pill had countered. 'Look at it like this. Without you, old Degenhardt won't put the Regiment back in the line. The longer you are away, the longer a rest the boys will get — and by God, they need it! Besides it can't do a young fellow like you any harm to blow his accumulated pay on wine, women and song — with not too much of the *song*!' he had added with a wink.

Surprisingly enough the divisional surgeon had agreed with the Pill and now, one week later, here he was in Berlin, confused, somehow out of place, and overcome by a sudden fear that he ought to be back where he belonged — with the Regiment. 'Wine, women and song,' he repeated to himself, automatically returning the salutes of the soldiers passing by in the slush, as he limped along with the black and white enamel medal of the Knight's Cross of the Iron Cross at the throat of his shabby frontline tunic. 'Where indeed does one get such things?' It seemed an age since he had last had a woman —

and somehow the veiled society women who passed in their long official Mercedes and looked invitingly in his direction did not appeal. He was not in the mood to be lionized and shown off at some society lady's salon for the admiration of gushing females and fat-bellied, pompous rear-echelon stallions.

Suddenly von Dietz wished he had never come to Berlin.

'Welcome to the slaughter-house,' Professor Hausser said, as the ugly nurse ushered him into the surgeon's big uncomfortable office at *la charité*. The office smelled of ether, cigar smoke — and fear. The big doctor with the balding head rose and gave von Dietz a firm and long handshake which seemed to suggest that the surgeon was not only welcoming him but testing his pulse and circulation as well.

Almost as if to confirm the Colonel's thoughts, Professor Hausser stepped back a pace, one hand still on the officer's skinny shoulder and said abruptly, 'Is your father Chinese, Colonel?'

'What ... what was that, Professor?'

Hausser repeated the question and von Dietz said, 'No, of course not, Professor.'

Hausser beamed at him, showing a mouthful of gold teeth and indicated he should sit down in the leather chair opposite his desk. 'If that's the case then, you have a mild case of jaundice. Nothing to worry about though. It's the diet and strain at the Front. With the fatless diet you'll get here at home, it'll soon go away of its own accord.' He glanced briefly at the papers in front of him on the desk and said, 'All right, take off your boot and roll up your trousers so that the butcher — me — can have a look at your flipper.'

Obediently von Dietz did as he asked.

Hausser sniffed as he caught sight of the old scars from previous wounds which marked the Colonel's leg. 'I say, you really have earned your piece of tin,' he indicated the Knight's Cross at von Dietz's throat.

Von Dietz said nothing and turned his outstretched leg so that Hausser could get a better look at the ugly purple wound, which was now beginning to heal.

Hausser crossed over, glared at it as if somehow angry, tested von Dietz's knee, bending it and then twisting the kneecap painfully a couple of times before saying, 'You're going to have trouble with that leg for the rest of your days, Colonel, if you're not careful.' Slowly he walked back to his desk and sat down.

'So I've already been informed by my own MO, Professor.'

Hausser rested his chin on his clasped hands and stared at the younger man. 'Colonel, with your leg, you could get six months here in Berlin having specialized treatment. Think of what that would mean to a handsome young fellow like you, on full pay in the capital as an out-patient with none of your dreary hospital routine. Once a day to the slaughter-house for a little bit of manipulation and water treatment by a pretty young nurse.' He puffed out his cheeks. 'Where could you get a better offer than that in this year of 1943?'

'Where indeed, Professor!' von Dietz said with a laugh. He was getting to like *Herr Professor*, *Dr* Peter Hausser. 'But I'm a regular officer, Professor. War means promotion, you know. Sometimes even generals get killed in wartime. One has to seize the opportunities as they come.'

Hausser's smile vanished. 'War means death, von Dietz,' he said. 'I've already lost one boy at the Front and I have two others in the East. Good God, don't you think I'd use every trick in my power as a doctor to pull them back here to Berlin if I could? The war's lost, von Dietz. After Stalingrad everyone with the least bit of common sense must know that,' he contorted his face bitterly. 'Of course, our leaders have lost contact with reality. The Gift-Dwarf talks of total war and final victory. Absurd! It would be better if we sued for peace now. But our masters won't hear of it.' He shrugged. 'So, my dear Colonel, it is *sauve qui peut*. Therefore, I would suggest the following to you. Do as I did as a young officer when I used to come on leave to Berlin from the trenches in the old war. Check yourself in at the Hotel Adlon, if it's still standing with these damned terror raids of the British. Blow all your pay — you must have plenty of it coming to you — find yourself an expensive whore and fill yourself and her with champus. Then come back to me in a week's time and let me know what your decision is. Then, if you wish, I'll see that you are written sick — *permanently*!' He rose to his feet and stretched out his hand. 'That's it, Colonel. Now I must be off, back to the slaughterhouse. I've got a bit of butchery to perform in the operating theatre in half an hour's time. Good-luck, and remember,' he added, his wise old face suddenly grim again, '*this war is lost...*'

'There is no doubt about it, my dear Colonel,' the golden pheasant with the beer belly and World War One decorations on his splendid tunic, rumbled confidently, placing his hand on von Dietz's knee, 'the summer offensive in the East will change the situation completely.' He beamed at the soldier. 'Then these defeatists and nervous nellies here in Berlin will have to eat their words. Believe you me, the Führer knows what he is doing all right. He's biding his time. All we can do to help him is to keep our nerves.' He clicked his fingers at a passing waiter, an old man in a rusty frock-coat who creaked as he walked, '*Herr Ober*, two whiskeys for me and the Colonel,' he ordered.

The waiter halted. 'No whiskey left, *Kreisleiter*,' he croaked, showing his ugly, ill-fitting false teeth.

'No whiskey left! My God, what is the Adlon coming to? After a day's hard work for the Fatherland, one would think a decent hotel could offer a fellow a glass of whiskey. All right, make it a brandy — and a French one, mind you. None of that muck made in the Rhineland.'

'*Jawohl, Kreisleiter.*'

The golden pheasant winked at von Dietz. 'They make the brandy down there out of Jewish piss — *dead* Jewish piss.' He smiled hugely.

Von Dietz frowned coldly. He didn't like the man. But that wasn't very strange; he didn't like anyone at the hotel. They were all provincial Party officials up in Berlin for some conference or other, or high-ranking government officials living there while their families had been evacuated to the country away from the bombing. To a man they were all confident that Germany would win the war, confiding in him when they were drunk — which seemed to be most of the time — 'enjoy the war, old chap, peacetime is going to be terrible.'

Von Dietz looked at his watch. In half an hour, Wanda, the whore, would be arriving for another dinner, drinks and bed afterwards. He couldn't stand her during the daytime — her incessant chatter about money bored him to tears — and preferred to wander through the city, telling himself that it seemed another world from the Front, in spite of the fact that its once-confident citizens were now beginning to feel the first impact of the war as the British stepped up their bombing. He sighed and wished she would be early tonight so he could get away from this bore.

The ancient waiter came with the brandy on a silver tray. The golden pheasant looked at the label of the bottle suspiciously. 'You're sure that's Martell?' he growled.

'This *is* the Adlon, *Kreisleiter*,' the waiter answered, looking down his nose.

'All right then,' ungraciously the golden pheasant accepted his glass and waited until von Dietz had taken his. He raised his drink to the third button of his elegant tunic, arm extended rigidly at the elbow, as if in some caricature of a Prussian officer at the turn of the century. 'To victory in 1943, Colonel!' he barked so loudly that here and there heads turned to stare in wonder. Von Dietz said nothing. Instead he raised his glass and took a careful sip.

The party leader frowned. 'You didn't respond to my toast, Colonel?'

Von Dietz shrugged.

'Don't you believe in victory in 1943 then?' he rasped.

Von Dietz returned his accusing look calmly. '*Kreisleiter*, I am not paid to *believe*, I'm paid to *fight*.'

'But belief is the basis of successful combat, Colonel.' There was an icy note in the golden pheasant's voice now. 'All of us in the Party know that. It is essential that our nation believes if we are —' he stopped short.

From far away there came the first thin, frightening wail of the air-raid sirens. The steady 'tick-tock' note of the radio link, which' was kept running all the time in the Adlon as in every other public place in the Reich these days, changed to an urgent 'ping-ping', the signal for enemy bombers over German territory. In the hotel lobby all conversation ceased. People went pale. Over in the corner the ancient waiter poised in the middle of pouring out a drink for a guest, his head cocked to one side, waiting for the announcer to break in.

The 'ping-ping' stopped. The silence was intense. '*Achtung, achtung!*' the announcer barked, his voice full of dread and urgency. 'Large formation of enemy aircraft heading for Berlin. Enemy air-raid on the capital expected...'

The rest of his words were drowned by a sudden rush of guests for the stairs leading to the cellar. The golden pheasant swallowed his brandy in one gulp, grabbed his gold-braided cap, and joined the throng. '*Victory in 1943?*' von Dietz called after him maliciously. But the official was too frightened to hear or to react; he was too busy fighting his way to the front of the crowd, blustering and cursing as he did so.

Now the waiters and other staff ran back and forth, turning off the main lights and opening the windows to prevent them being smashed by the blast. Now von Dietz could hear the sirens wailing outside quite clearly and the first heavy thumping of the 88mm flak guns at the outskirts of the capital.

The ancient waiter who had brought the brandy tapped him on the shoulder. 'Excuse me, Colonel, but you must go.'

'Must I?'

The waiter nodded solemnly. Of all that elegant crowd, he, alone, seemed unafraid and in full control of himself. 'It's police orders. Everyone has to go to the cellars —' he stopped abruptly. There was an ominous drone overhead and through the open window, the two of them could see the first multiple flares coming down. 'Christmas trees,' the waiter said . 'They'll be dropping their eggs in a few minutes, the English gentlemen of the Royal Air Force. You'd better go.'

'*The English gentlemen of the Royal Air* Force' did it. Von Dietz told himself one couldn't argue with a man like that. He finished the last of his brandy and reached for his cap and cane. 'I'm off. Thank you and good luck to you.' 'Good luck to you, too, sir,' the waiter called after him, standing there in the middle of the elegant lounge, as if he had all the time in the world. Von Dietz limped to the door and out into the glowing Berlin night.

Now the whole horizon to the east of the city was ablaze with a pink light, streaked with the incandescent flares which were dropping everywhere. Men and women were running frantically for the shelters, stark terror on their faces. Buses, trams and cars stood abandoned, their engines still running. Whistles shrilled. Frightened shouting people, burdened with bundles and rucksacks, fought to make their way into the shelters.

Von Dietz hesitated. He did not like the idea of going into a shelter packed with terror-stricken humanity. But the streets were emptying rapidly and soon some officious warden or *schupo* would be sure to order him to get under cover. He frowned and looked around for a suitable place. Then he saw the glowing blue sign of the *U-Bahn*. The Underground, that would do it; there would be more room there to escape the stink that frightened civilians gave off. He forced his way down the stairs already crammed with shouting people and wailing children and found himself on the over-crowded platform.

'Can't stay here, Colonel,' a man in the uniform of the Storm Troops said. 'Try tunnel C.'

He nodded and pushed his way down to the next platform. Here, too, the civilians were jammed tightly together, strangely silent now, their pale faces expressing their intense fear; for the British bombers were now directly overhead.

There was a dull thud: The sound of splintering glass. A wave of acrid explosive came down the tunnel. Von Dietz standing there with the motionless silent crowd thought they looked like people viewing a solemn funeral. 'Perhaps their own,' a little voice inside him said. Suddenly von Dietz was glad there were no small children near him. He could not have born the looks on their pale faces, so unnaturally quiet.

There was a series of shrill whistles — one, two, three — the bombs crashed down just above the tense crowd. The tunnel vibrated frighteningly. Mortar trickled down in a grey rain as a great cloud of smoke came sweeping down from the shaft.

The crowd panicked. As one they surged forward towards the stairs. The Storm Troopers were swept aside as they tried helplessly to bar the throng's way up. 'Don't move!... It is forbidden to leave the tunnel!' they cried. Von Dietz was carried along with the rest. His cane was wrenched from his hand and he yelped with pain, as he brought his full weight down on his wounded leg. 'Here, hang on to me!' a voice cried next to him. 'Give me your hand!'

In the half darkness, now full of the choking fumes of burning timber, he grabbed the skinny shoulder offered him, using his free elbow to force his way forward, trying to avoid stumbling over the cases and rucksacks which the crowd was now abandoning in their panic. And then suddenly they were outside and blinking furiously in the bright scarlet glare of the blazing buildings all around, the heat making them gasp as if with shock, tearing the air out of their very lungs, while the flak thundered mightily, sending glowing red fireballs into the burning sky above Berlin. 'Thank you,' von Dietz turned to his companion for the first time, then exclaimed, 'you're a woman!'

The tall pale-faced girl with the long blonde hair swept down low over one green eye laughed drily. 'So I have been told. Come on! Let's get out of this mess before it's too late!'

'No more shelters!' von Dietz cried, as opposite a tall office block started to fall apart, its masonry coming down in a blazing avalanche.

'No more shelters… My cellar. *Now hurry!*'

Supported again by the girl, they fought their way through the crazed confusion around them, trying to ignore the screams coming from people trapped in the ruins. Charred shrunken corpses littered the streets, bodies hung from trees like human fruit, a horse clattered crazily round a corner, its mane and tail on fire, followed by a crazed howling dog. Then a gas main exploded to their right and like a gigantic blow torch its searing flame shot house-high into the sky. Covering nostrils against the stink of singed hair, they passed a group of soldiers sorting out the charred bodies of children. Hysterically weeping women watched as the little bodies were loaded into trucks.

'Didn't I tell yer,' one of the soldiers said to his companion, as he tossed a little girl's body effortlessly onto the heap sprawled in the back of the nearest truck, 'that firestorms finish off everything and everybody, mate.'

'I heard them screaming,' a woman said, shaking uncontrollably. 'If there was a God, he would have shown some mercy on the poor mites.'

Next to her another woman, hard-faced, dry-eyed, who looked half-mad in the eerie flickering light said harshly, 'Leave God out of this, woman. God doesn't make war, *men do…*'

In the candle-lit cellar they made love savagely, almost brutally. The dying city outside forgotten as they writhed and tossed on the wooden bunk, gasping, groping, grunting in greedy passionate abandon.

When a bomb slammed into the earth close by and sent the whole cellar quivering with its impact, raining tiny flakes of plaster on their naked sweat-lathered bodies, they did not notice. Magnified and distorted by the wildly flickering flame of the candle, they continued their crazed frantic dance, consumed by a fever of love...

'They're dying everywhere now,' she whispered, her flushed face dripping with sweat, as they squatted there naked, smoking and listening to the thin bitter wail of the 'all clear'. 'Men, women, little children ... dying everywhere in Berlin.' She said the words without emotion, as if she were making an observation about the state of the weather outside. The girl — he didn't even know her name — moved him a little. In a way she had awakened in him the sense of privation which afflicted all front swine. In the frightened revulsion from death at the front they all turned instinctively to the act of love to make them feel whole again. Sometimes it was sticky sentimentalism, sometimes it was gross sexual obscenity; but in essence it was the same thing. Afterwards the women would be forgotten as completely as if they had never even existed. Women were irrelevant in the harsh savage world of the Front. But for the time being this woman's abandoned pathos moved him.

'It won't go on for ever,' he said automatically.

She brushed the long blonde hair back from her damp forehead. 'It will,' she replied, her voice breaking, 'until we're all dead. You, me, everybody. They will have no mercy. *All dead in Berlin! In Germany! The whole...*' she flung open her arms, her tiny breasts rising with them, the nipples suddenly taut again. He reached out for her. 'Don't talk!' he commanded, smothering her words with his hungry lips. Almost brutally he forced her down on the wooden bed once more...

'As far as the *Wehrmacht* is concerned,' the fat medical officer with the purple stripe of the staff down the side of his elegant trousers, was pontificating, 'syphilis means the loss of a fighting soldier for thirty-seven days and gonorrhoea for twenty-nine days. Of course, our brothels behind the lines are well organized. But you can't ensure that the men won't visit others. Most unfortunate...'

Professor Hausser grinned and closed the door, cutting off the medical officer's complaints. 'Everywhere you go these days, Colonel,' he said, 'it's *sex, sex, sex!*' He indicated that Colonel von Dietz should sit down, and added, 'I see you're walking without a cane again. Now I regard that as a bad tactical move.' He grinned once more, though his eyes behind his tortoise-shell glasses were wary and not a little worried.

'Bad tactical move?'

'Yes, Colonel. If you're going to go before the medical board, you must make the right impression. Scrim-shanking is a serious business you know, a cane is usually regarded by the professional malinger as a useful adjunct.'

Von Dietz laughed softly. 'Oh, I see what you mean now, *Herr Professor.* But I don't think I shall be needing the cane for that particular purpose anymore.'

Hausser hesitated before he spoke. 'Didn't you have a good time in Berlin then?'

'I don't quite know, Professor. I took your advice on the whore, who was costly but very satisfactory, and the last two nights I have spent in a cellar with another girl, a nice girl *once* I imagine, though now,' he shrugged and didn't finish the sentence. 'On the whole,' he continued trying to make a joke of it, 'the Front is safer than here in Berlin. The RAF is making life here very dangerous you know, sir.'

'I know, Colonel, I know,' Professor Hausser said solemnly, his gaze taking in every feature of the hollowed, hard face in front of him, as if he were trying to see something there, known only to himself.

'Seemingly these days a fellow can get killed back at home.' He stopped short. Professor Hausser was clearly not listening to him.

'You're going back aren't you, Colonel?' Hausser said.

Colonel von Dietz nodded.

'Everybody fiddles, scrounges, malingers, tricks, betrays, lines his own pockets these days, von Dietz,' Hausser snapped, suddenly angry, his dark eyes blazing behind the thick lenses of his glasses. 'Here at home and probably at the Front, too. The whole structure of our society is corrupt, from top to bottom. Our orderlies pinch the patients' rations from the kitchens and sell them on the black market. The doctors steal the drugs. Even our famous Sauerbruch compromises himself — not for what he *does*, but for what he *doesn't* do.' Professor Hausser waved his hands angrily. 'The whole damn lot of us are crooks. Why should you be different? Why should you go to the Front and get your silly head shot off for the likes of us, eh? Tell me that, Colonel, pray!'

Colonel von Dietz's head snapped back under the impact of the sudden attack, as if the doctor had struck him a physical blow. 'I ... I don't...'

But Hausser wasn't listening. 'Do you not know that you are helping to perpetuate an evil system, you and all the rest of you brave fools at the Front? The longer you continue to fight, the longer *they* will survive, plunging us ever deeper into the morass, ruining our beloved country irrevocably. Don't you realize that heroes like you with those cheap enamel medals for bravery around your necks are better off at home, taking the backbone out of the Front so that it's manned by second-raters, cowards, potential deserters, crypto-communists and God knows what else — anyone at least who values his own neck first and his country second? Let the Russians force us out of their country, into Poland, and then back to where we started from — Germany — so that our leaders are forced to make peace while we've still got a Fatherland left! Let... He broke off helplessly, chest heaving with the effort of so much impassioned talking. 'Von Dietz, I beg you, for your sake and your country's — *don't go back to the Front!*'

Slowly von Dietz shook his head. 'I am a von Dietz, Professor,' he said without emotion. 'The von Dietzes have served Germany loyally for more than two hundred years, whether their political masters were right or wrong. I agree with all you say, but I must continue to serve, whatever the outcome. Thank you, Professor, for your attempts on my behalf. But I must ... go back...'

'Then damn you! Go back and get yourself killed!' Furiously the Professor scribbled something on the paper in front of him and thrust it at von Dietz. 'Take it, your discharge from *la charité*. Go and get yourself killed. I wash my hands of you.' He glared down at the desk.

Slowly von Dietz got to his feet and limped to the door. He paused as if to say something; then changed his mind and left without another word. *Professor Dr* Hausser did not look up...

He sat there in his room in the Adlon, smoking idly and watching the pale blue smoke rise against the darkening sky. At midnight the troop train was to leave for the Eastern Front. The management had kindly allowed von Dietz to keep his room until then 'without any extra charge, Colonel,' the dapper little greasy man behind the counter had assured, adding in a lower voice, 'and if der *Herr Oberst* would like one of the ladies-of-the-night to keep him company for his remaining time in Berlin, I am sure it can be arranged.'

But von Dietz did not want the company of a 'lady-of-the-night' or anyone else for that matter this evening. Somewhere someone was playing a piano softly. He did not recognize the melody, but he enjoyed its rippling silver spray of notes, happy for a while in this limbo between home and the Front, momentarily plunged into a deep pool of stillness against the soft cascading music. Thus he sat there, a tall lean man, watching the smoke rise, listening to the music, thinking...

CHAPTER 2

Under the shattered glass-roof, the loudspeakers boomed, echoing the length of the crowded platforms, with below the gigantic black locomotives steaming and clanking, as if impatient to be off on their long journeys eastwards. '*Special troop train via Breslau … connections Lvov, Warsaw, Vinitza, Brest-Litovsk, Smolensk…*' The harsh impersonal voices chanted the names of the places which would soon mean death for most of the men in field-grey who swarmed everywhere, laden with equipment and thick winter clothing. Colonel von Dietz, watching them with mild curiosity from the window of his compartment, thought they looked like arctic explorers setting out on a long expedition into the unknown. '*Planned departure zero twenty-three hours, forty minutes… All personnel will board at zero twenty-three, thirty…*' the voices droned on, occasionally being cheered by the drunks who were reeling around everywhere under the hard gimlet gazes of the chain dogs. The station-master appeared in his high-peaked red cap and cross-belt, followed by the RTO officials with their checkboards and pencils, walking the length of the long train, writing mysterious numbers in chalk on the side of the carriages and wagons. The women knew it would not be long now. They started to sniff and dab their eyes with handkerchiefs. Their grey-clad menfolk began to make embarrassed 'tut-tutting' noises and the red-faced drunks, standing alone in their ripped tunics, jeered.

Reluctantly the soldiers began to break away from their women and moving through the steam that was now flooding the platform towards the train, they seemed to be walking into a thick fog.

Von Dietz, settled comfortably now on the wooden seat, had seen it all before. These scenes of tearful leave-taking no longer moved him, he found them embarrassing.

'*Abend, Herr Oberst, gestatten?*' the harsh incisive voice at the door made him turn sharply.

An officer in the black uniform of the Armed SS stood there, poised, his hat set at a rakish angle over a cheerful, bold face, a black patch over his left eye, his left sleeve tucked neatly into his belt. His tunic was ablaze with decorations. Behind him a little man with the look of a Siberian, heavily laden, dressed in the nondescript grey of a POW auxiliary , waited patiently. '*Obersturmbannführer* Drexler, may I enter, *Herr Oberst?*'

Von Dietz grinned. He liked the look of the man; he was a front swine like himself. 'Surprised you asked, Drexler. Thought you fellows of the SS just took what you wanted. The name is von Dietz.'

The SS officer grinned. 'In one of my more charitable moods, von Dietz, I suppose,' he barked. 'The savage beast that lurks in my breast has been calmed for a while. Well, come on, Igor, don't just stand there like a wet fart waiting to hit the wall of the thunderbox — break out the champus, man, or by the Great God and All His Triangles, I'll send you back to Uncle Stalin!'

The little Siberian servant gave an apprehensive shudder and hurriedly dumped the officer's kit, before opening a box packed with ice in which reposed six bottles of dripping champagne. 'Champus, sir,' he lisped and hurriedly began to pull off the silver paper.

'Oh leave it to me, you little asparagus Tarzan,' Drexler snapped, 'I'll do it!... Shit in the wind now!'

As the servant departed hurriedly, Drexler finished pulling off the foil and tossed the bottle to von Dietz. 'Yours,' he said, and pulled another one out of the ice-case for himself. 'Should last us till Breslau at least. Then we can start on the schnaps. Got another case in the rear.' With a grunt he cracked the neck of his bottle off and took a deep drag at it, spitting out glass splinters as he did so.

Outside on the platform, the self-important station-master adjusted his peaked cap and blew his whistle. It echoed down the platform with an air of sad finality. Immediately the locomotive's steel wheels chattered frantically, steam hissed out with a roar, and the chain dogs, hands on rifles, marched forward, intent on preventing any last minute deserter escaping.

'*Good bye, Willi... Mind how you go, Horst... Try not to get your feet wet, Karl... Write at once... Think of me... I'll be true... GOOOOD ... BYYYE...!*'

The hysterical cries of women and the hopeless cries of their men merged into one great meaningless moan of despair and longing as the long troop train started to edge slowly from the platform, every rivet and strut groaning and straining with the effort.

Drexler spat out some more glass, belched and sat back in his wooden seat with a happy sigh. 'Thank God,' he said. 'Thank God that's the last of Germany for a bit... Life at the front is simpler for a poor old stupid hairy-arsed stubble-hopper like me!' He raised his bottle in a toast to the officer sitting opposite him, his eyes blank of emotion. '*Prost!*'

'*Prost!*' von Dietz returned the toast, telling himself that the SS man was right. Germany 1943 was simply too complicated for a simple soldier...

Solemnly the brass band on the platform intoned the *Death March*. Black-clad officers of the SS stood at attention, looks of mock sadness on their faces as the stretcher was wheeled up on top of a personnel carrier.

'Home sweet home, *Obersturmbannführer*,' Drexler said thickly and with his last bottle of schnaps indicated the pink flush of the permanent barrage to the east. 'Bye, Horst.'

'Bye, Kuno,' von Dietz grinned, as Drexler staggered to his feet, clambered down the little steps and collapsed into the waiting stretcher.

Sadly his fellow officers who had come to welcome him back saluted and one stepped forward to place a wreath of fir branches on Drexler's chest. 'All we could get, Kuno,' he apologized.

'At least you could have had a bottle of firewater waiting for a chap after the dangers and hazards of the Home Front,' Drexler complained and with a wink at von Dietz closed his eyes, hands folded as if in prayer across his bemedalled tunic. The parade swung round and to the sad strains of the *Dead March* Drexler was borne off back to his regiment.

Von Dietz shook his head and next instant wished he hadn't. It had been a very boozy three days. Gratefully he took a deep breath of the good clean Russian air. Then, as the whistles shrilled and officious transportation officials bellowed orders, the leave men began to reluctantly form up. The death machine had them in its grasp once more.

'*Horst!*' that well-remembered voice broke through von Dietz's hangover haze.

He swung round. The Pill was standing at the far end of the crowded platform, waving his arms excitedly. Von Dietz grinned. Good old Pill! It was typical of him to make the long uncomfortable journey from the coast by truck to meet him. He swung his rucksack and started to elbow his way through the throng of miserable, lethargic soldiers waiting to board the trucks which would take them back to their units.

'Pill ... Pill, you old dog!' von Dietz exclaimed happily embracing the grinning MO, while at the door of the truck Deltgen stood to attention smiling his welcome. 'How goes it?'

'Excellently, excellently,' his old friend replied. 'For once we're not up to our hooters in the crap.'

Von Dietz relinquished his hold on the other man and shook Deltgen's hand. 'The fodder all right, Deltgen?' he asked, as he swung himself into the cab together with the Pill.

'*Prima*, sir!' Deltgen replied, as enthusiastic as the MO. 'None of your old roof-hare and giddi-up soup, but real tinned Old Man and every second day a piece of salami. The quartermaster bulls even broke down and cooked us a roast last Sunday,' he thrust home first gear and honked his horn to clear a group of miserable-looking soldiers out of the way. 'Though old Red Rudi maintains that he found a bit of horseshoe in his piece. But you know him, sir, he's allus crying stinking fish.'

'Indeed, I do,' von Dietz said as the big truck started to bump its way onto the frozen highway and past the first group of freezing auxilliaries, who guarded its length against the threat of partisan attacks. He turned to the Pill. 'What's the situation at the Front?'

The Pill frowned and the happiness vanished from his weathered face. 'I suppose I could cheer you, Horst, by saying it's quiet. But in my opinion, it's *too* quiet.'

'What do you mean?' von Dietz asked as they rolled by the still smoking remains of a burned-down cottage, with two roughly made birch-wood crosses standing beside it. The obvious result of some recent partisan attack. 'How — *too* quiet?'

'Well, once we withdrew, as you know Friend Ivan followed us up and occupied the positions we abandoned.'

Von Dietz nodded.

'But then he stopped. That I consider strange. You would have thought that Friend Ivan would have pushed home his advantage, instead of just sitting on his thumbs doing nothing.'

'Agreed,' von Dietz said thoughtfully, his headache forgotten now. 'If he had played his cards right, he might have rolled up the whole Front in this sector.' He changed the subject. 'And what of the gentlemen of Divisional Headquarters, Pill?'

'Nothing much. Degenhardt has been making noises as usual — but nothing urgent.'

'If I may say something, sir,' Deltgen said, carefully negotiating a shell-hole in the road.

'You may, you rogue,' von Dietz said, suddenly feeling happy to be back among his own people, regardless of what might come.

'It's not really a buzz, sir, not even a latrine-o-gram,' Deltgen said with unusual care. 'But when you've got a long hooter like me and the other old heads, you can almost smell it.'

'Smell what?'

'That there's something in the air. The fodder, for one thing, is getting better by the day, and even those kitchen bulls can't nick the amount of grub they're sending down from Div. Then the other goodies they're pumping us full of, like cigars and vodka.' He winked knowingly and hooted at a skinny-ribbed dog that was about to cross in front of him, 'They're fattening us up for the kill, sir, mark the word of an old head. It won't be long now before they're sending us in for the chop again...'

As the days passed in the little seaside resort where the 69th Regiment was resting, von Dietz came to realize soon enough that most of his men shared Deltgen's opinion. Time and again he caught little groups of them strolling along the promenade, talking quietly together, their brows furrowed, a hint of desperation about their faces. And there was little drunkenness, although as Deltgen said, there was a plentiful supply of vodka coming down from Division. Yet in spite of the general apprehension, he noted that they still retained a faith in each other, believing that as long as they stuck together somehow things would work out all right.

The letters which he and the other senior ranks censored before the men could send them home confirmed that they feared they would soon be going into action again. The letters also revealed a feeling, however crudely expressed, of isolation, of disconnection with time and home, as if the writer felt compelled to finalize his worldly business just in case...

By the end of the first week, Colonel von Dietz had begun to agree with his men. There was something in the wind! Division was revealing nothing, but twice they had received a visit from Degenhardt's Chief-of-Staff who had asked apparently casual questions about the state of the Regiment, and once the Divisional Surgeon had spent a whole afternoon with the Pill, discussing the sick cases and the general health of the Regiment.

In the second week, the first of the newly-healed lightly-wounded had been returned from the Divisional General Hospital, followed a few days later by a draft of eight hundred 18-year olds, straight from the Reich training schools; young boys who gaped open-mouthed at the old heads as if they were creatures from another world.

In the same week, von Dietz and the Pill were out riding on two Siberian ponies which Sergeant-Major Bulle had 'organized' for them, when they heard the curious shrill crawling sound of a fife-and-drum band coming from the other side of the hill to their front. Intrigued they had spurred their shaggy little mounts up the rise to see below a rolling wave of infantry on the march. Mounted officers rode at the front, followed by the pipe band, and finally the trudge-trudge of heavily laden infantry. A thin blue wave of pipe and cigarette smoke hung over the seemingly endless column like a pale spirit.

There must have been two regiments, von Dietz estimated in the end, two whole regiments. They were followed by the rumbling box-like horse-drawn ambulances and the smoking black goulash-cannon drawn by *panje* ponies.

The Pill had looked at von Dietz as they sat there watching the long, grey crawling snake below, but had said nothing. Yet von Dietz had known what he was thinking: those reinforcements were not being brought up to sit on their bottoms in the frontline. They would be going into action, offensive action.

Thus he was not altogether surprised when one bright, spring Monday morning, General Degenhardt himself made an appearance at his HQ.

'Great God,' the Pill exclaimed, looking out of the window and seeing the grey Mercedes wallowing heavily through the black mud which was everywhere now that the ground was beginning to thaw, 'it's the Div. Commander — and we haven't even got his own personal thunderbox dug!'

Von Dietz laughed. It was a standing joke throughout the Division that Degenhardt had a horror of the usual communal latrine and everywhere he went insisted on a special one being dug for him and placed under the guard of an officer so that no one else could use it. 'Doubt if he'll be staying here long enough for that eventuality. Bulle!'

'Sir?'

'Turn out the guard and see that they present arms properly. You know what a stickler the General is for such things.'

'Sir!'

Von Dietz hastily buttoned up his tunic and adjusted his belt, as outside the guard snapped to attention and the General, beaming all over his fat face, hurried through their ranks, hand raised to his cap.

He waited till Bulle opened the door for him and strode in confidently, the new Knight's Cross he had received for von Dietz's defence of Height 560 bouncing up and down at his throat. 'Well, my dear von Dietz,' he said exuberantly as von Dietz and the Pill snapped to attention, 'how good to see you again — and you too, Doctor! Recovered, I see. Splendid!' He nodded to Bulle. 'You may go, Sergeant-Major.' Bulle gave him an impressive salute and departed, while the General waited, tapping his foot impatiently, hardly able to conceal his excitement. Then it burst out, 'We've got it, von Dietz! We've got it!'

'What, sir?'

'A lovely new battle, my dear fellow! Straight from Corps. There'll be tin in it for everybody.' His little eyes sparkled. '*The Division's going over to the attack once more...*'

CHAPTER 3

General Degenhardt's mental processes were easily followed. His mind was not stirred by great tactical or strategic problems. He was more concerned with seeing that soldiers were well turned out and didn't stub out their cigarettes in fire-buckets. He loathed paper work and had little idea of maps. Von Dietz had seen him often enough staring sulkily at a map, fat sausage-like fingers hesitant as they hovered over it, while he waited for his clever chief-of-staff to come to his aid and explain what had to be done.

But today there was no chief-of-staff there to help him and he had to explain the plan he had just received from Corps himself, growing progressively more crimson in the face as he did so; for he was an officer who knew his own shortcomings and normally protected himself at Divisional Headquarters with clever men, who did his thinking for him.

'As Corps sees it,' he spluttered, 'the Popovs have worn themselves out in front of Leningrad. They haven't the strength to take the offensive here this spring at least. So,' he looked at von Dietz a little hopefully, as if he half-believed that the younger officer might do the explanations for him, 'we shall attack first — and catch them off balance.'

Von Dietz said nothing, his face remained stony and unrevealing.

'Er, because if we wait they'll come at us sooner or later,' Degenhardt continued a little unhappily. 'A further attack is inevitable. Therefore Corps thinks we must beat them off the mark.'

'Does Corps?' Von Dietz said ironically. But irony was wasted on General Degenhardt.

'Yes. General Lindemann stated last week at a meeting of all corps and divisional commanders — and I quote, von Dietz — "The liberation of Leningrad will always be an important goal of the Bolsheviks. The Soviet regime equates the liberation of Leningrad with the defence of Moscow and the battle to retain Stalingrad".' General Degenhardt, a little happier now that he could use thoughts already formulated by someone else, continued, 'and General Lindemann also stated that the final liberation of Leningrad will be regarded by the Popovs as a second Stalingrad and that the Führer has stated categorically that there will *not* be a *second* Stalingrad this year!'

'I think, General, that the Führer is no longer in a position to decide whether or not there will be a second Stalingrad, as you phrase it,' von Dietz said.

'I did not hear that remark, von Dietz. Now hand me that map of the Front, please.'

The Pill, knowing what was running through his comrade's mind and knowing too that the slightest thing might well push him into an open confrontation with this fool of a general officer, picked up the map himself and placed it in front of a frowning Degenhardt.

Degenhardt placed his stubby, fat fingers on the map, his pudgy face sulky and quite without intelligence. 'Our main Corps attack will go in here between Mga and Pulkovo. Intelligence thinks that is the axis between the Popov Leningrad Army and the Volkov one. Usually the weakest spot in any Front, as you know, von Dietz.'

The Colonel said nothing and Degenhardt stumbled on. 'Now we of this Division have been given a particularly juicy mission of our own. From Oranienbaum we are to launch a seaborne assault on the coastal resort of Streina, just behind the Popov line. It will serve, according to Corps, as — one, an important feint and diversion; two, if it comes off, as a possible means of rolling up the whole of the Popov flank. Then, of course, Corps will reinforce us with fresh troops and…' His voice trailed away, as he finally noticed the look on von Dietz's face. 'What's the matter?'

'*Seaborne*! Did you say *seaborne*?' von Dietz exploded, his lean face flushed and angry, while at his side the Pill waited anxiously, ready to interfere at once, if Horst went too far.

'Yes, I did.'

'But how in God's name are we going to have the least chance of success in a seaborne operation, General? Don't you realize the untold difficulties involved? The fact that troops have to be specially trained in assault landings from the sea. The fact that our fleet in the Gulf of Finland do not possess the special landing craft we'll need. The fact that it is more than likely the Russians are well-dug in with heavy artillery at such a tactically important spot. The fact…' He gave an angry shrug. 'In three devils' name, General, there are a myriad difficulties!'

Degenhardt tried to bluff it out. 'Corps thinks you have a seventy-five per cent chance of pulling it off.'

The Pill noted that ominous 'you', but said nothing. 'Naturally, all means available will be put at your disposal, and the *Kriegsmarine* have promised their fullest co-operation, von Dietz.'

'You say "you". You mean, of course, my Regiment?'

'Yes, von Dietz, the 69th is my most experienced regiment and after consultation with Corps, it has been decided that your regiment will be given the honour of making the initial seaborne assault.' He looked up at von Dietz's taut, angry face more hopefully.

Von Dietz swallowed his rage with difficulty. 'General,' he said, 'I do not regard the task of sending my men on what may well be an Ascension Day mission as an honour. The 69th has a long and honourable tradition on the battlefield. But its commanders have never attempted the impossible — at the expense of its men's lives.'

Degenhardt flushed. 'You have my word, von Dietz, that you will be given the fullest possible support to ensure that your attack will be a success. My word on it!'

Von Dietz said nothing. 'Besides, a soldier must obey orders without question. That has always been the basis of our army in Germany, von Dietz. Corps has ordered me to carry out this mission and I shall carry it out. I order you and you will obey that order — or,' General Degenhardt hesitated only momentarily, 'face the consequences.'

Instinctively the Pill tensed. Horst's reaction to this threat was unpredictable. But he need not have feared, for now von Dietz was in full control of himself. 'General,' he said, 'I am as much a coward as the next man. Naturally I shall obey your order. I don't want to end up like poor General von Sponeck , but,' his voice was suddenly harsh and incisive, 'I want full operational control, and the power to make the ultimate decision on the spot.'

'And what's that supposed to mean?'

'This. If when we have landed, I think the opposition is too great and there is no real chance of success, I want the Navy to evacuate us at once. This will mean that you will have to ensure the Navy doesn't turn tail and run for port as soon as they have deposited us on the beach at Streina.'

'But I couldn't … couldn't ask Naval HQ for something *like that*, von Dietz!' Degenhardt exploded. 'The Admiral would go up the wall. You know how those damned sailors go on about their precious ships. They … they'd…' Von Dietz waited calmly until he had finished spluttering and then taking the General's arm said, 'Come with me, sir. I want to show you something.' Firmly he steered the General to the window and with his free hand rubbed the condensation away so that they could look out.

'Those are my heroes — my chaps — General. Have a good look at them, please.'

Bewildered, General Degenhardt stared out at the men in shabby field-grey, chatting quietly in small groups, hands in pockets, small clay pipes or cigarettes sticking out of the corners of their mouths, the features on their lean faces pared down to the bone by the lives they had been forced to lead at the Front, their eyes, even here in comparative safety, somehow wary and on their guard. 'But what am I supposed to see, von Dietz?' he blustered.

'The looks on my heroes' faces, General.'

'Well, they look like one expects front swine, as I believe you call yourselves, are supposed to look.'

'That they do, General. And that, too, is the only loyalty they possess — to others of their own kind, other front swine. *Not* to Division, *not* to Corps, *not* to Army, *not* even to Germany, but only themselves and their comrades!'

'But I really don't understand where all this is leading, von Dietz!'

'I shall tell you,' von Dietz replied icily, leading the bewildered general officer away from the window. 'When Count von Sponeck withdrew his division contrary to orders and thus saved many hundreds of lives which might well have been wasted if he had held on to his position as commanded, he was foolish enough — because he was an honourable man — to allow himself to be separated from his division. Once he had made that mistake, the authorities could deal with him as they wished.'

'I still do not see where —'

'I will not do you or Corps that service,' von Dietz interrupted the red-faced General firmly. 'And I have the utmost confidence in my men, even those of the new draft. They will back me up to the hilt, if I wish to take a stand against orders which I think will endanger their lives.'

'But that would be … mutiny!' Degenhardt breathed. 'Exactly, my dear General — mutiny in *your* Division!'

Degenhardt swallowed hard. 'What are you saying?' he breathed, his voice hoarse.

'This. Either you get me that naval support I have just requested, or,' he hesitated only for a fraction of a second, 'I shall order my men to refuse all commands. Then instead of one poor Count von Sponeck facing the authorities by himself, you will have me, plus two thousand men disobeying you and meeting whatever charges you might be prepared to lay against them.' Colonel von Dietz lowered his voice, knowing instinctively that even Degenhardt was beginning to realize what that would mean. 'And my dear General Degenhardt, you simply cannot hide two thousand men. Think what effect a mutiny of that kind would have on your further career in the *Wehrmacht*? There will not have been anything like it since the bad old days of 1918, eh?'

The Pill flashed von Dietz a look of admiration. Of course! That was the way to ensure that this new operation had a half-way chance of success. The High Command, most of whose generals had served on the Western Front in the old war, had a horror of repeating the events of that terrible year of defeat, when whole regiments, divisions, had mutinied and torn off their officers' epaulettes and badges of rank, humiliating them disgracefully. For the older generals it had been a traumatic experience. Any field commander who allowed his soldiers to mutiny in this war would certainly be speedily relegated to the 'Führer-Reserve' of unemployable officers.

'But Colonel von Dietz, you couldn't...'

'I *could* and I *would!*' Horst cut into Degenhardt's bluster. 'Now are you going to ensure that — one, I make the decision on the spot and two, the Navy will be waiting there off shore ready in case I decide to evacuate?'

Degenhardt let his fat shoulders slump in defeat. 'It's blackmail, Colonel...'

'*Are you?*'

Degenhardt nodded his head in dumb defeat.

'Thank you, sir. I shall have a detailed plan of attack at your HQ within the next twenty-four hours, sir!'

Five minutes later General Degenhardt's car had disappeared the same way as it had come, with the General slumped moodily in the back, not even acknowledging the ritual of the 'present arms' which normally so absorbed him.

The Pill nudged von Dietz. 'Horst, you rogue, you told the fat shit, you really did,' he said enthusiastically. 'You handled the situation magnificently. You should have been a diplomat, you know.'

'Or a blackmailer,' von Dietz added with a wry smile. 'All the same, Pill, I'm not happy, not happy at all. Landing my poor old stubble-hoppers by boat against opposition which we know nothing about — only the Greater German High Command, in all its vaunted wisdom, could think up something like that.'

'You have given your promise, Horst,' the Pill reminded him. 'Besides you can't push old Degenhardt too far. That particular worm would turn too, if he thought his fat head was in danger.'

'I know, Pill, I know. The only people we can trust is ourselves, the front swine.' He shrugged. 'Oh well, I must get down to planning, but believe you me, the 69th has finished taking risks.' He jerked his thumb at his skinny chest. 'From now on, we front swine are out for number one and God can piss on the rest...'

CHAPTER 4

The little Admiral with the bright blue eyes dug his hands deeper into his pockets as he glanced around the excited young faces of his torpedo-boat skippers. There was no fear at the impending action on their faces, nor any of the war weariness and cynicism of the gentlemen in field-grey. His skippers relished the idea of the coming scrap, however dangerous it might be.

'Good,' he barked, as if he was addressing a quarterdeck and not the wardroom, 'let's begin, eh.'

There was an excited murmur of agreement from the smooth-faced young ensigns and lieutenants, which brought a well-meaning smile even to von Dietz's harshly handsome face.

'Now, gentlemen, I'll not underplay the dangers. We know little of these waters, the shallows, the currents etc. They're bound to be mined, and naturally Leningrad's shore defences are formidable.' He glared at them with those blue eyes, as if he were challenging one of his excited listeners to say the mission was not dangerous.

'However, gentlemen,' he continued, 'we have two factors on our side. One, the Reds won't be expecting us to attack. Two, at this time of the night, we'll be in and out — hopefully — before they have collected their vodka-befuddled Red wits. Now, what's the plan? I'll tell you. Phase one. In go the fly-boys from the *Luftwaffe*, to make a hell of a racket and drop their square eggs on the thick Red skulls. Well,' he gave his listeners a crooked grin, 'they'll *attempt* to drop their square eggs on target, but knowing the gentlemen of the *Luftwaffe*, I have my doubts.'

There was a ripple of laughter from the other officers crowded into the smoke-filled heaving wardroom. There was no love lost between the *Kriegsmarine* and *Luftwaffe*, von Dietz told himself.

'Main thing is, they make a din to cover up you chaps of the torpedo-boat squadron,' the Admiral went on. 'Phase two, you fellows go in through the shallows off Oranienbaum to provide the feint these field-grey jobs will need. If you see a target of opportunity, all the better. Let 'em have a tin-fish up its bottom. We could use a few kills to show old Dönitz in Lorient that his high and mighty submariners are not the only fellows in the Navy fighting this war.' He sniffed and turned his bright blue gaze on von Dietz standing there with his battalion commanders and the Pill. 'Phase three, Colonel, you and your field-greys. All things being equal and with a bit of luck, the noise the *Luftwaffe* makes and our diversion should cover your landing. We'll get as close to shore as we possibly can. Can't have your delicate-chested chaps getting their feet wet, can we?' He smiled at von Dietz, but his eyes remained hard and piercing. Suddenly von Dietz liked the little Admiral with the pugnacious chin and bold challenging face. He was a refreshing change after Degenhardt and the rest of the careerists back at HQ. 'Now,' the Admiral continued, 'I'm putting in a couple of my destroyers to cover the landings — just in case. But the trick is, naturally, to get you ashore without any firing whatsoever, what?'

'Exactly, sir. The further we can get inland without being spotted, the better. If we're pinned down on the beach, we're in trouble, real trouble.'

'I understand,' the Admiral barked. 'Now only one thing more. *If* you run into trouble and have to be brought off, this is the drill. I emphasize that *if*, Colonel, because I am not one who likes to envisage the possibility of defeat right from the start, even before the operation has started.' He glared hard at the Colonel.

Von Dietz nodded, feeling he could rely on this man.

'Well, this is the way we'll do it, *if* Radio-link codeword — S.O.S.' He grinned suddenly, showing a mouthful of dingy, sawn-off teeth, as if he might file them down before each breakfast. 'Meaning not what you think, Colonel, but — the "shit's on the shingle"!'

There was a burst of laughter from the assembled officers and as tense as he was, von Dietz smiled and laughed too. The Admiral was a card.

'If your radio's knocked out — and these things do happen, Colonel, then signal rockets, two green flares, a white and a red. Got it?'

'Yessir.'

'Good. And remember the Reds are cunning arses: use the rockets one time only, because if you use them twice, they'll cotton on and try it on with signals of their own. Finally, *if* we have to pull you out, it'll be done under the cover of my guns. I'll bring up my cruisers to give the Reds a really big pain. Gentlemen, all that remains for me to do now is — one, tell you to circumcise your watches. It is exactly zero one hundred hours! Two, wish you all luck. Three, invite you all to partake of a very large rum and black tea before you go to your battle stations.' As if the chief steward had been listening behind the wardroom door, it opened right on cue and white-coated stewards started to file in, bearing silver trays on which rested glasses of steaming tea, giving off the thick heady smell of Jamaica rum. The Admiral winked at von Dietz, '*Style!*' he barked above the excited chatter.

Von Dietz winked back and said, 'Style indeed!' Suddenly he felt reassured and safe. The Navy certainly did have style and efficiency. Things were going to go all right...

A thin dreary grey mist hung over the harbour approach. It clung in wet patches to the shrouds of the ships moving silently through the still water, making their rigging look bearded. Now a heavy brooding silence hung over the crowded little fleet, broken only by the plaintive cries of the night birds.

Von Dietz, shivering a little in the damp, raw, cold body, heavy with equipment, eyes trying to peer through the gloom, wondered about the men grouped all around him. What were they thinking at this last moment? As they clasped the hard coldness of their weapons, did they long for the softness of a woman's belly and the wiry warmth of her pubic hair? When they hitched up the heavy stick grenades to place them in their boots ready for instant use, did they compare their unyielding weight with that of a woman's breasts seized greedily from behind?

All of them had women waiting for them — sisters, mothers, girlfriends, wives — knitting and writing to them, sending them parcels, waiting for their letters, worrying about them, being faithful, being unfaithful... Were they thinking of those women now and if they were, how could they accept their fate? Why didn't they simply fling down their weapons and cry out — 'No, I'm not going to do it. Never!'

But, of course, they wouldn't. Soldiers never did. A little angrily he dismissed the thought of women. It was annoying how women came creeping into the crevices of the mind at the most impossible of moments. He concentrated on the landing.

Now at the bow of the leading barge which carried his own HQ, the bosun started to sing out the depth in a soft bass, while the soldiers tensed, the weapons they held now wet with sweat. And above them on the open bridge, the young lieutenant with his white cap tilted at a rakish angle, gave soft unhurried instructions to the helmsman.

Behind them, the rest of the barges crawled through the grey gloom at a snail's pace, their bows hardly making a ripple in the dark-brown sluggish water.

Von Dietz flashed a look at the green-glowing dial of his wristwatch. In five minutes the *Luftwaffe* attack was scheduled to go in; they would be followed almost immediately by the crazy young skippers of the torpedo-boat squadron. He uttered a silent prayer, hoping the noise and feint would cover his landing, for if there was any opposition waiting for them over there on the barely seen beach, they would be slaughtered in the shallows. Now with his eyes, ears, and every muscle strained with tension, von Dietz felt his nerves beginning to sing out in electric protest.

Suddenly, frighteningly, a finger of icy white light stabbed the grey gloom to their right. The soldiers caught their breath. The bosun froze, lead hanging foolishly from his hands. '*Verdammte Scheisse!*' the lieutenant on the bridge cursed as the searchlight started to swing round slowly in their direction. '*Shit!*' Red Rudi whispered to Deltgen, as the light wavered for an instant, as if the operator thought he had spotted something in the grey dripping murk but wasn't quite sure whether or not his eyes were playing tricks on him. 'Couple more minutes and the Popov bastard'll spot us!'

Now the beam had commenced moving again, parting the grey gloom and advancing upon them relentlessly, ready to pinion them in its eye-searing glare.

But it wasn't to be, for suddenly the lethal silence was shattered by the roar of many engines.

'*Thank God for the Luftwaffe!*' Deltgen cried as the bombers came roaring in at tree-top height, and the whole coast erupted in the thunder of flak guns. In an instant the searchlight flicked away from them, its harsh white light clearly outlining the torpedo-boats racing across the bay, prows raised high, seeming to hit each individual wave like a brick wall.

All hell was let loose. Orange flames shot up everywhere. Tracer started to scud over the water, dragging burning red flame behind. Machine-guns chattered. Bombs started to whistle down. Star-shells exploded in crazy profusion. In an instant all was chaos and confusion.

Now there was no longer any need for silence in the barge fleet. At the top of his voice the bosun commenced singing out the depths and the young lieutenant shouted his instructions to the helmsman.

'Prepare to land!' von Dietz cried, buckling on his helmet. He turned to the Pill, his old face grim and set in the reflected light, eyes wary under the rim of his steel helmet. 'Now, take care of yourself, Pill,' he said and stretched out his hand. 'There aren't many sawbones like you who warm their flippers before they give the boys their short-arm inspections.'

The Pill grinned warily and pressed von Dietz's hand. 'Look after yourself, Horst. I couldn't stand the strain of breaking in another regimental commander — at my age.'

Von Dietz returned his grin and then strode to the railing. The flat-bottomed barge was gliding to a halt. 'Stand by, you riflemen!' he barked, trying to ignore the rattle of massed Soviet machine-guns to their right. Meanwhile the torpedo-boats snarled and roared along the coast in huge bursts of wild white water. 'Sergeant-Major Bulle, get ready to follow me!'

The Bull swallowed fearfully. 'Sir,' he croaked and touched the steel shaving mirror that he had pushed down the front of his trousers as a rough-and-ready form of protection against the worst kind of wound a man could suffer. 'Riflemen, stand by!' The leading barge ground to a halt. 'One metre, skipper!' the bearded bosun sang out, raising his dripping line out of the still water.

'That's it, Colonel!' the skipper cried down from the bridge. 'From here on, you walk!'

Someone farted contemptuously and said, '*Swim*, you mean, if we're unlucky, sonny boy.'

Von Dietz grinned as he tugged himself over the side. The boys were keeping their nerve all right. He tensed himself for the impact of cold water and dropped.

The shock took his breath away. The water was freezing. His boots ground against the gravel of the bottom and shivering furiously, all sensation gone immediately in his lower limbs, he started to wade ashore.

Now all up and down the beach there was the metallic clank of steel on steel as men began to come over the sides of the barges and wade ashore, cursing when they hit the water or slipped on the shingle.

Von Dietz stamped up the wet sand. Near Leningrad, the bombing had reached its height and flames were shooting high in the air, drowning even the snarl of the torpedo-boat engines. Von Dietz stamped his leaden feet to bring some sort of life back into them and looked at the dark shapes, silhouetted starkly against the flames, as they struggled through the water, weapons held high above their heads. The landing was going beautifully. So far there hadn't been a shot fired at them from the dark hinterland. Evidently Friend Ivan had been caught completely off guard, or the combined air and sea raid had fooled him. He whispered an order to Bulle and the riflemen, and then taking one last look at the fog-shrouded water to confirm everything was going well, turned and started to stamp inland, followed by the tense riflemen under Sergeant-Major Bulle.

The beach seemed very dark after the glare out to sea. Twice von Dietz stumbled and almost fell on the wet cobbles, as he walked forward, counting the paces, telling himself that the beach might well be mined.

At two hundred paces, which he calculated would be about eight metres and still no mines, he stopped. 'Bulle, hold the men here. You two,' he indicated Red Rudi and Deltgen standing behind the massive NCO, 'follow me.'

'It's allus the little blokes who land in the shit,' Red Rudi grumbled.

'Get off, you miserable bastard, do you want to live for sodding ever?' Deltgen snapped. 'Do as the CO tells yer!' Von Dietz grinned in the darkness and then holding his free hand in front of him to protect his face against the trees and broken rock beyond the beach, he started off. The two comrades followed.

Minutes passed leadenly. In the little wood the sound of the battle off Leningrad was muffled by the dripping, miserable, stunted trees, and suddenly the three of them felt very much alone and isolated. Instinctively, and although as veterans they knew it was wrong, they bunched together as they crept forward, parting the wet branches as if they were curtains which might well reveal some frightening apparition the very next moment.

Now the firing seemed very far away. For all they knew, they might have been alone in the world. Von Dietz took his bearings, while a soft wind came in from the sea and stirred the trees, dripping drops of moisture onto their bowed helmets.

He thought he saw a piece of road leading off to the left. If this was so and if it was the one he had marked on the map twenty-four hours before, it was the one they wanted. The road leading into the southern part of their objective, Streina. But in this hazy grey light objects were deceptive, and von Dietz couldn't be sure. At his side he heard Red Rudi and Deltgen shuffle their feet uneasily and knew he had to make some sort of decision. 'All right, Deltgen, get back to the beach. Tell Sergeant-Major Bulle to signal the Admiral we are advancing on our objective. Tell him, too, to pass the word to the three battalion commanders to follow. The beach isn't mined and there's no opposition — *yet.*'

'Right, sir,' Deltgen whispered and slung his rifle. Then as an afterthought just before he left he turned severely to Red Rudi, 'And you watch out for the Colonel, Rudi, or I'll have the eggs off 'n yer with a blunt razor-blade!'

'Piss in the wind, arse with ears!' Red Rudi hissed, but without rancour.

Von Dietz grinned, and said, 'Come on, yer rogue. Let's go and see if we can earn our pay this day.' Then they were gone like grey timber wolves and Deltgen hurried back through the fog the way he had come ...

The little Admiral read the signal and then handed it back to the flag officer. 'So far so good, Hansen,' he snapped, feeling the ship heel under him as she turned, heading back with the rest of the little fleet for the safety of the open waters of the Gulf of Finland.

'What now, Admiral?' Hansen said.

The little Admiral shrugged and sipped at his cold tea and rum. 'We wait, I suppose, Hansen... What a dull business war is, don't you think? It's virtually ninety per cent waiting and ten per cent action. And after one's waited for so long, the something that happens is never what one expects. I suppose in the end your average soldier learns to wait and expect nothing. That's known as patience.'

Hansen smiled down at his commander. It was the first time that the dynamic little man, who never seemed to be able to sit still for a moment, had ever philosophized in his presence. 'If I may be so bold, Admiral, we are very thoughtful tonight — I mean, this morning.'

The Admiral looked at him hard, the bright blue eyes unblinking.

'Don't like it, that's why, Hansen.'

'Don't like what, sir?'

'This op, Hansen. It's gone off too easy, too damned easy! There must be something wrong somewhere.' And with that cryptic statement *der Herr Admiral* turned to his cold tea and relapsed into a gloomy silence…

CHAPTER 5

The Russian attack came suddenly. The first cautious riflemen of the 69th Regiment were approaching the main street that ran straight through Streina when they heard the nerve-shredding *brhh-brhh* of a Russian automatic metres away. The leading rifleman dropped his weapon and it clattered to the cobbles. He fell himself a second later without a sound. The man behind him screamed and clutched a bloody shoulder. At once the darkness was stabbed by knives of scarlet flame on all sides.

Now automatics and machine-guns opened up to their front and left rear. A soldier running past von Dietz in panic took a burst in the stomach and fell screaming, arms stretched out in front of him. Another was hit to his left and was whirled round furiously like a dancer by the impact. Von Dietz shrilled the alarm on his whistle and fell to one knee, desperately trying to assess the situation. A soldier sprang over him, and the next instant lay there moaning, pawing the cobbles in his frenzied agony.

Frantically von Dietz raised his machine-pistol and sprayed quick inaccurate bursts at the upper windows to left and right. There was the sound of splintering glass. A scream. A body fell from a window to the right and hit the cobbles like a sack of wet cement.

There was the obscene belch of a mortar. He could hear the shell howling through the pre-dawn sky, ripping it apart furiously. *'Into the houses!'* he screamed. *'Take cover, for Chrissake, take —'*

The shell exploded to his immediate front in a ball of vicious red flame. The blast slapped him hot in the face. He felt the air ripped from his lungs. Gasping for breath, he knelt there, head bowed, as if at prayer, listening to the shrapnel and debris rain down on his helmet.

The stunned men of the 69th were now smashing at the windows and doors of the nearest houses, hammering crazily at the woodwork with the butts of their rifles, desperate for cover. The Regiment started to take more and more casualties. Von Dietz still crouched in the middle of the main road waited in agony, watching his brave men fall, as the concentrated machine-gun fire and that of the lone mortar ripped into them. My God, why were they taking so long to get under cover? If they didn't hurry, there soon wouldn't be much left of the 69th. The wounded and dying men now lay on the cobbles everywhere.

To his left a man was groaning pitifully next to a steaming new crater in the road. He crawled towards the moaning man, the tracer cutting the air lethally just above his head. The man saw him and started to drag himself forward on his elbows, without raising his head, his legs obviously shattered.

Von Dietz stretched out his hand. 'Grab my hand, I'll tow you!' he called above the chatter of the machine-guns.

The wounded man raised his head, his eyes already covered with the glaze of death. It was Dietrich, the commander of his Second Battalion. There was no suffering on his face, in spite of his moans, only a sort of stupefaction. 'Colonel,' he gasped, his lips rapidly turning white, indicating death wasn't far off, 'get 'em out … get 'em out! We've walked into a trap… *Get 'em…*' His face slapped into the cobbles. He was dead.

Now the Russians were getting bolder. They were beginning to come out of the houses, bayonets fixed. The mortar had ceased firing, for fear of striking its own men. But von Dietz's men, who had finally succeeded in breaking into the houses, were starting to react. Lying there near the dead Major, von Dietz immediately recognized the controlled firing of well-trained men. They had overcome the panic and surprise of the trap that had been sprung upon them. To his front, Russian after Russian now fell.

Von Dietz suddenly became aware of his own danger. There was nothing more he could do for the wounded sprawled out on the cobbles. He'd have to make a run for it. He rose to his feet and cast a wild glance to left and right. To his immediate right, a Russian appeared and with amazing calm slowness raised his rifle and pointed it at von Dietz.

The Colonel didn't give him a chance to fire it. He dived forward. The butt of his schmeisser hit the muzzle of the Russian's rifle. It tumbled from the man's grasp and the two of them collapsed together on the ground. A broad, unshaven peasant face stared up at von Dietz, transfixed now by absolute fear. The officer clubbed his fist and brought it down cruelly on the man's nose. It smashed like pulp. The Russian howled in agony. Von Dietz felt his hand wet with blood. Carried away by fear and fury, he smashed down his clubbed fist once more. Something snapped audibly. Blood spurted from the Russian's ears. He gave a little yelp like that of a puppy dog and lay still. Next instant von Dietz had grabbed his machine-pistol and was pelting for the cover of the nearest house, followed by a fury of Russian bullets.

'What time is it?' one of the riflemen asked, leaning against the hastily improvised barricade of cupboards and tables propped against the window.

'Who the hell cares,' Red Rudi snarled. 'All I know it's my birthday. I'm twenty-five today.'

Deltgen winked at Colonel von Dietz slumped wearily in the corridor. 'Many happy returns. What a nice day you picked, Rudi!'

Red Rudi made an obscene gesture with his middle finger. 'Sit on that, you shitting garden-dwarf.'

'No can do. Rudi. Got a bus up there already,' Deltgen replied easily.

Von Dietz forgot the patter between the two old heads and concentrated on his problem, while outside in the body-littered street a wounded Russian whimpered like a hurt child. They had been trapped in the houses for two hours now and in that time, he reasoned, the Russians must have worked their way behind him on both flanks. However, he was still in contact with his Third Battalion and they were still holding the beach, though the radio link with the fleet had been severed. The question now was should he hang on to the edge of the town in the hope that Degenhardt's two remaining regiments would be able to break through and link up with him; or should he attempt to fight his way back to the beach and wait for the fleet to pick him and his men up as soon as it was dark enough? It was a damnable decision to make., A fighting retreat in broad daylight with very little chance of coordinating the attempt beforehand was not the kind of tactical operation he relished, particularly as they would be burdened with the wounded too; at all costs he would not leave his wounded behind. The acceptable solution at the war academy would be, under such circumstances, to play safe and wait for Degenhardt to link up with him. But could he trust Degenhardt? 'Operator,' he called to the slightly wounded radio-man nursing his bleeding hand in the corner well away from the enemy slugs which kept chipping the paint off the walls, 'I want you to raise General Degenhardt's HQ for me, please.'

'Sir,' the operator replied, while von Dietz stared through the shell-hole in the roof at the sky which was now filling with great black rain clouds. There would be a storm soon, he told himself.

'Ready now, sir. In clear?'

'In clear, operator,' von Dietz snapped. 'No time to put it into code now. Too late for that. All right, here we go. To General Degenhardt...'

That morning the great surprise attack along the length of the Leningrad Front started to come to a halt. Within hours of the troops leaving their positions, they found themselves bogged down everywhere, slogging it out with fresh and superior Red Army units so that by midday the signal rockets requesting help and assistance were dotting the sky the length of the German line.

Later the generals explained to the Führer that the whole plan must have been betrayed by spies to the Russians. It was a convenient fiction which convinced Hitler and saved their own careers, for the time being. But that midday, with the storm clouds rolling in ever thicker from the sea, the corps commanders and divisional generals were apprehensive and downright frightened, in some cases, as the ever more alarming messages came flooding into their headquarters and the telephones rang incessantly, demanding artillery, fresh troops, instructions. Everywhere worried, white-faced staff officers carried on the best they could, exhorting, pleading, threatening, lying, promising, cajoling — anything they could think of to prevent the Front breaking completely — while they waited and sweated that overwhelming decision that their particular 'Old Man' had to make: *fight on, or call off the great attack*!

It was no different at General Degenhardt's divisional headquarters. There, too, anxious staff officers ran back and forth, while telephones jingled and mud-splattered dispatch-riders roared into the courtyard below bringing ever fresh tidings of woe from neighbouring units, and urgent pleas from the two regimental commanders poised at the far left of the line for instructions.

As always General Degenhardt played his bluff, hearty, fat-man role, which he believed inspired confidence in his white-faced officers — and procrastinated. For in truth, he did not know what to do. If he failed to attack, he would run the wrath of the corps commander and if he did under existing circumstances, he might well lose his division; and General Dirck Degenhardt had not sweated out a quarter of a century of miserable military life on poor pay and poorer rations in order to lose his first divisional command. At his age he wouldn't get another chance, he knew that. So he paced back and forth, trying not to look out of the window at the confusion below in the thick black mud, while in Streina Colonel von Dietz's regiment bled to death.

In the end it was Kraemer, his Chief-of-Staff, who took the bit between his teeth and approached the fat sweating General. For HQ had just received a desperate von Dietz's message requesting a decision on the fate of the 69th. 'General,' he snapped, not quite able to conceal his contempt at the fat fool, 'you must do something, you know, before it's too late.'

'What do you mean, Kraemer?'

Kraemer did not pull his punch. 'You know Lindemann will have to go on account of this fiasco. A couple of corps commanders will probably go with him. Believe you me. By tomorrow the High Command will be howling for blood and a few heads will roll.' He paused heavily, and then added, 'You understand me, General?'

Degenhardt's poise collapsed immediately. 'Do you mean I'm in danger of losing the Division?'

'You certainly are, General.'

Degenhardt looked almost tearful. 'But it's not my fault that the 69th has run into trouble over there,' he pointed one of his sausage-like fingers in the general direction of the east.

'And I'm not alone. Other commanders are in trouble too, as you well know, Kraemer.'

'Self-pity stinks!' Kraemer said harshly, ignoring the General's comment. 'And it's not going to do you much good when you're living at Berchtesgaden on half-pension and digging your garden as your main form of occupation, is it?'

'But what can I do, Kraemer?' There was a note of pleading now in Degenhardt's voice and his jowls trembled fearfully, as he looked up at the tall, immaculate, hard-faced staff officer. 'I can't do anything yet because Corps hasn't passed on the order to call off the attack. The plan still holds.'

'It does, General — *for fools*! For once you have to use your own initiative and stop those two regiments before they attack. The gentlemen of the High Command will take no excuses for failure.'

'But what of von Dietz's regiment, Kraemer? If there is no link-up, he'll pull back.'

'So?'

'So, the Navy will be forced to evacuate him and his men. Do you want me to be responsible for a large-scale sinking of naval vessels which might well take place in such an operation? God in heaven, they'd slaughter me at High Command if that happened. You know how those admirals go on about their precious boats, as if they paid for them personally or something.' General Degenhardt stared at Kraemer, his face a mixture of despair and hope.

Kraemer considered a few moments. At the far end of the big room, an ashen-faced staff officer was saying over and over again in a shaken voice, 'I repeat, *nothing* can be done, absolutely *nothing*.'

Finally the big Colonel spoke. 'This is the way we will do it, General. One, you will immediately order the two regiments to stand-fast.' He ticked off the point on his finger with its elegantly manicured, tinted nails.

Degenhardt nodded numbly.

'Two, you will radio C-in-C Fleet that there will be no further use for his ships. The 69th Regiment has coordinated its position and is digging in. There will be no evacuation.'

Again Degenhardt nodded.

'Three, radio von Dietz that he has full authority to make his own decision about the further employment of his regiment. Due to the present tactical situation, he is empowered to decide himself whether he stands and fights, or retreats back to our own lines.'

Degenhardt licked suddenly dry lips, but still he did not say anything. He waited until Kraemer finished.

'So you have saved most of your division, not involved the admirals and their precious ships, and if von Dietz loses his regiment, which is highly likely, that cannot be blamed on you. If he stands and fights, he will be a hero and still lose his regiment. If he runs away, he will be a coward and take the consequences — if he survives — and still lose his regiment, *without you being responsible*, General,' Colonel Kraemer emphasized the last words, his eyes boring into General Degenhardt's.

'But those soldiers of von Dietz, they'll be slaughtered,' the fat general quavered, suddenly deflated, appearing somehow smaller and thinner.

Kraemer looked down on him, his hard face drawn in a contemptuous sneer. 'They're front swine, aren't they, Degenhardt?' he rasped. 'If they are not slaughtered this day, then they will be on the morrow. That is the fate of front swine — it always has been.' He clicked to attention. 'General Degenhardt, I await your orders, sir,' he barked formally. 'You will give them orally and I shall ensure they are taken down in writing.' Colonel Kraemer was no fool. He clicked his fingers and a young staff officer hastened up, pad at the ready. If anything went wrong with the new plan, Kraemer was intent on making sure that Degenhardt, the fat idiot, would take full responsibility.

In a broken voice, Degenhardt began. 'Time, zero thirteen hundred ... priority one ... signal Colonel von Dietz... In view of the present situation at the Front, you are empowered by me...'

Kraemer smiled to himself. No longer listening, he strolled slowly to the big French window. His post was safe for another day. On the horizon the sky flickered with the first forked tongue of lightning. Soon there would be a great storm...

CHAPTER 6

'Heaven, *arse and cloudburst*!' von Dietz exclaimed angrily above the chatter of the Soviet machine-gun, busy chipping off the facade of the building in which he sheltered. He dashed the flimsy to the glass and cartridge-case littered floor. Hastily the radio-man who had brought General Degenhardt's message disappeared into his safe corner, still nursing his bleeding hand.

'Well?' the Pill demanded, rising from the man whose shoulder he had just bandaged up, and wiping his bloodstained hands on his trousers. 'What is it, Horst?'

'A bucket of shit, that's what it is, Pill!' von Dietz snapped. "'*Full authority to act on your own initiative! Fullest confidence in you! Best of luck! Degenhardt.*'" He quoted the radio message in angry bursts, his lean face flushed a furious red. 'You know what that means, don't you, Pill?'

'Yes, the old fart has lost his nerve once more.'

'Exactly. And now we've got to bathe the shitting baby!' Exasperated beyond all measure, he cried, 'Sergeant-Major Bulle, knock that sodding m.g. out will you! I can't damn well hear myself think with that racket going on!'

'Yessir,' Bulle quavered fearfully and gingerly taking up the sniper's rifle dropped by the man who had been wounded in the shoulder, crawled cautiously up the bullet-pocked wooden stairs to the upper storey where — with luck — he'd find someone to do the dangerous job for him.

'It's as obvious as the nose on your face, Pill,' von Dietz continued, controlling his anger a little now. 'The plan's gone wrong and he's stopped the attack to link-up with us. Now he gets out of the mess he's got us into by giving me full responsibility.'

'In other words, he's absolved himself from any guilt if things go drastically wrong.'

'*If* von Dietz bit back. 'They *have* gone drastically wrong. The question is —'

'What now?' the Pill butted in, as above them the sniper's rifle cracked sharply, once, twice, three times and the noisy Soviet machine-gun stuttered to a stop. There was the muted sound of cheering.

'Yes,' von Dietz cast a quick look through the hole in the roof. Lightning stabbed the sky in a scarlet zig-zag. A fresh wind lashed the shattered lathes and sent the broken tiles clattering to the cobbles outside. 'It's a damnably difficult operation to break off a fight in daylight, but I can't risk a night-withdrawal, not with the wounded and communications being what they are. Friend Ivan would slaughter us.'

'You're going to withdraw?'

'I have no alternative. It's back to the beach and then the Navy can take us off from there…' his voice trailed away and he looked enquiringly at the Pill. 'What's the matter, you old quack?'

The Pill forced a laugh, though he had never felt less like laughing. 'I was just wondering about those Navy boys. Nobody wants to be associated with a failure, not in this year of our Lord 1943. Stalingrad has been a nasty lesson for all branches of the service. Think of the beating old Fat Hermann and the *Luftwaffe* took over the business of the re-supply of Stalingrad and —'

'Piss or get off the pot, Pill!' von Dietz interrupted his old friend crudely. 'What in three devils' name are you trying to say?'

The Pill looked down unhappily.

'Well, come on, spit it out!'

'It's the Navy, Horst. I mean this evacuation is going to cause them losses.' He hesitated, his face suddenly miserable. 'Will they in the final analysis be prepared to risk having their ships sunk in what might well be a lost cause?'

The little Admiral jutted his jaw and thrust his hands even deeper into his pockets as the last of the torpedo boats came racing in, trailing a graceful curve of bright white water behind it. Its bridge was marked with the fresh gleaming silver scars of Soviet hits and there was a tangle of shot-off rigging aft, but the white-capped young skipper standing on the bridge under the black skull-and-cross-bones flag that the torpedo boat squadron affected, was grinning broadly.

The grin somehow annoyed the watching Admiral. Tell that young fart to con his boat better next time, Flag!' he snapped as the throaty roar of the torpedo boat's engines gave way to a steady throb.

'Will do, sir,' the Flag Officer snapped and doubled away to carry out the irate Admiral's instructions.

The naval mission had been completely successful. They had landed the grey jobs without a casualty and according to the returning torpedo boat skippers, who were already beginning to celebrate noisily in the white-painted casino just off the jetty, they had 'scuppered' six Red batteries and probably sunk at least three or four lighters or small coastal craft. Rarely had an operation in the tight waters of the Gulf of Finland gone off so successfully.

The Admiral tugged at the end of his nose and expertly whipping off the dewdrop which hung there, flung it over the railing. It was a bad habit he had picked up as a young cadet from the rough-and-ready seamen of the Kaiser's Navy, and one which his wife back in Luebeck was always complaining about. But he couldn't ever break it. Besides it didn't matter much more, he told himself. After this war there would be little in the way of polite society to find the habit shocking.

He paced the little, scrubbed deck for a few moments, absorbed in his problem, hardly aware of the noisy rendition of '*Wir Fahren gegen Eng-geland*' coming from the casino and the calls of the diving seagulls which always reminded him of the cries of abandoned children.

In essence the operation had been purposeless. The grey jobs had failed to take their objective and would soon fall back to — '*To what?*' a hard little voice at the back of his mind asked, raising again that problem which had plagued him ever since he had received the signal from that fat fool Degenhardt that his ships would not be needed any further. It hadn't fooled him one bit. Thirty minutes later his own sources at General Lindemann's Army HQ had informed him that the whole attack was failing and that before the day was out, the Army would break off its new offensive. That meant that young Colonel and his soldiers would have to make a run for it.

Three years before he had been with the party that had accompanied Field-Marshal von Rundstedt to view Dunkirk after the Tommies had run away. He had never forgotten that beach dotted with abandoned vehicles, half-sunk in the shifting dunes, the fantastic twisted skeletons of burned-out carriers, and the still brown bodies lying everywhere, the feet in those big heavy boots the Tommies wore looking absurdly large in comparison with the strangely shrunken men. Hundreds of them, thousands of them, some of them nudged gently back and forth with the rest of the flotsam by the gentle waves. Even hard-drinking old Rundstedt had been moved. He had raised his skinny hand to his cap in silent salute and croaked in his ancient cognac-thickened voice, 'Poor fellows ... poor fellows. God forbid that anything like that ever happens to us!'

Now it was. The grey jobs didn't stand a chance. Once out in the open of the beach, the Reds would massacre them. Yet that would be the obvious thing for them to do — retreat to the beach and wait for the ships to come and pick them off. It had been planned that way in case of failure.

Now the plan had failed, but there would be no fleet to whisk them off to safety.

The little Admiral's bright blue eyes blazed fiercely and his hands balled to angry fists inside his pockets. It was all so damned unfair and cowardly. There was no official request from the Army for him to intervene; how then could he? Yet could he bother about such inter-service frills and courtesies when not a dozen sea-miles away hundreds of his fellow Germans were probably dying without a hope in hell? Wasn't he a German first and an officer of the German Navy second? Over at the casino the drunken torpedo boat officers had changed from the bold aggressive marching song of 1940 to the more apt and sadder song of 1943, '*Know That There Will Be A Wonder One Day*'.

The little Admiral shook his head. There were going to be no wonders this year. Everyone had to accept his inevitable fate. He turned, his shoulders suddenly hunched in defeat, and wandered miserably back to his quarters. He would order the chief steward to bring tea and rum and drink himself into temporary oblivion. There was nothing else he could do.

On the horizon, the first thunder rolled back and forth across the leaden sky in brooding ominous portent...

194

Outside the wind howled furiously, lashing against the bullet-pocked walls of the house in which they sheltered, drowning even the snap-and-crackle of small arms fire in the body-littered street outside.

Now it wouldn't be long before the storm broke in all its fury; and an anxious von Dietz waited for it to do so, knowing that it would give him the cover he needed if he were going to have any chance of bringing off his desperate escape plan.

Save for the handful of riflemen still firing back at the Russians, the rest had stripped off their packs and heavy equipment, keeping only their weapons, with the walking wounded crouched by the rear door waiting for the signal to go. At the radio the wounded operator crouched, relaying last instructions to the Third Battalion holding the beach and as yet not in contact with the enemy.

The Pill finished his last inspection of the wounded's bandages and nodded to von Dietz. 'They'll do, Horst — for a while at least.'

'Thanks, Pill.' Von Dietz clicked home his last magazine and automatically touched the single stick grenade tucked into his belt. Like the rest of his men, he was low on ammunition. If they got bogged down anywhere in their desperate attempt to escape from this trap, that would be it; they'd run out of ammo very quickly.

The thunder rolled and once more forked lightning stabbed the black rolling clouds. Von Dietz looked up. The first heavy raindrops splattered on his upturned face. On the stairs the grey kitten which had strayed into the house from God knows where scampered for shelter. Von Dietz grinned in spite of the tension. 'That's right, pussy,' he said, 'don't get your fur wet.' Then he was businesslike once more. 'Red flare, Sarnt-Major!' he barked.

Sergeant-Major Bulle crunched over the shattered debris on the floor and standing directly underneath the hole in the roof, raised the clumsy-looking signal pistol. He pressed the trigger. There was a soft plop and the red flare exploded above them, bathing their tense features in a blood-red, unreal light. It was the signal for the walking wounded and their escorts to move out. The rear door was flung open. The noise of the impending storm and the rattle of small arms fire grew louder. 'Out you go!' Von Dietz barked. 'And remember, make for that sunken road. Good luck!' 'Good luck to you, sir,' one rifleman, a boy whose right arm was gone, called back and von Dietz's eyes filled momentarily with tears. What brave fellows they were, he told himself. He couldn't let them down. He'd get them back — come hell or high water!

Now the wind was howling furiously about the house, buffeting it with a giant fist, making it shake so violently that Deltgen cried above the noise, 'Shit, the Popovs are bad enough, but now Mother Nature's trying to rub us out!'

Von Dietz smiled and yelled back, 'Not at all, you rogue! With a bit of luck she's going to save us ... Bulle, green flare!' While the Bull prepared to fire, von Dietz turned to the Pill, who would be now going out with the more severely wounded, following the first group to the sunken road. He stretched out his hand. 'I'm relying on you, Pill... Don't take any chances.'

'I won't, Horst. Don't forget, you can't get rid of weeds that easy.'

'Of course not, you old sawbones.'

The green flare exploded above the house and the Pill accompanied by the two riflemen who had been wounded in the leg and could only hobble left the same way as the others. Von Dietz breathed a sigh of relief. The sick and the lame had departed. Now the healthy ones would cover their withdrawal.

With a bit of luck they'd be able to sneak through the Russians to left and right along the sunken road. The storm would help. 'All right, men,' he cried above the howl of the wind and crack of thunder, 'let's give Friend Ivan some tinder!'

'I've only got one belt of ammo left,' Deltgen cried from where he crouched behind the MG 42, which he had taken over from the dead man slumped in a pile of brick rubble.

'Doesn't matter. We're not taking it with us. Let 'em have it.' He poked his machine-pistol through a hole in the wall. Outside the sky had become a great cliff of black cloud. Huge drops of rain were beginning to explode with ever increasing force on the body-littered cobbles in cold-white fury. The thunder was deafening. Somehow it seemed purposeless to fire against that background. But he did, snapping off slugs to left and right, seeing the bullets explode in vicious eruptions of blue and red sparks on the walls of the houses occupied by the Russians, with here and there white blurs of faces vanishing as the surprised enemy ducked for cover.

Now the last defenders poured a hail of fire at the enemy while the storm raged and the house creaked and groaned, as if it might come tumbling down at any moment. Mentally von Dietz counted off the minutes, restraining himself time and time again from giving the order to cease fire, knowing that the wounded would not make it so quickly to the cover of the sunken road.

'The signal, sir!' Bulle croaked ashen-faced from his position at the door.

Von Dietz swung round. Through the open door he could see the silver light of the signal flare, wavering and trembling through the hissing wall of rain. It meant the first party had reached the road, found it not occupied — so far — and were advancing to make contact with the Third Battalion.

The Pill and the more badly wounded couldn't be far off the road either by now. In five more minutes he would move out with the last defenders. 'Bulle,' he commanded above the racket, 'signal — five minutes to go. You chaps, start planting your mines!'

While the Bull popped the last signal cartridge into the bell-shaped muzzle of the flare pistol, the others began to place the home-made anti-personnel mines carefully among the rubble and debris.

'By the end of this day, there's gonna be a lot of Popovs who'll be singing sopranos,' Red Rudi said throatily, propping up the fiendish little devices in front of him so that when the Russian infantrymen burst into the house in their usual fashion they would stand on them. Instantly the charge would explode driving the loosened slug straight into their groins.

Deltgen shuddered dramatically, 'Christ, Rudi, don't even think such things!' He cursed. 'Imagine having yer crown jewels shot off! *Scheisse*, gives me the willies just —'

'Silence!' von Dietz cut into his outburst, cocking his head to one side tensely.

All of them obeyed their CO's command immediately. Desperately von Dietz strained his ears, trying to make out the sound against the fury of the storm. Was that really the high-pitched unmistakable hiss of a German MG 42? 'What do you think, Bulle?' he called to the huge NCO crouched near to the open door.

'It's our lads, sir. Can't mistake that MG 42.'

'Is it the Third. Battalion, sir?' Deltgen called from his position at the wall.

'Yes, Deltgen. It's our only chance. If they can convince Friend Ivan that we're making a determined attempt here, they might draw off — for a little while. Then we can make a run for it.'

'To the beach, sir?'

Von Dietz shook his head, telling himself as he began to explain that never in his whole wartime fighting career had he ever embarked on such a desperate operation with less than a twenty per cent chance of success. 'No, I'm hoping the Russians will think we are going to do that and act accordingly once they've recovered from their surprise at the Third Battalion's attack.'

'*Where* are we going, then, sir?' Deltgen persisted.

'Back to our lines — through their front.'

Deltgen looked at his running-mate, his face aghast. Slowly he began to cross himself, something which he had not done since the day he had been confirmed in Cologne Cathedral.

'All right, break up the weapons we're leaving behind. We're off in exactly sixty seconds,' von Dietz snapped.

As the men ripped out the bolts of the automatic weapons and smashed their firing pins on the bricks lying everywhere, von Dietz started to count off the seconds. On the stairs the kitten stared at him with grey solemn unwinking eyes. Outside the storm raged furiously, the thunder rolling back and forth across the heavens deafeningly. Von Dietz threw a last glance at the kitten seated there so safe and self-assured. Suddenly on impulse, for reasons unknown to himself, he picked up a brick and threw it savagely at the animal. It fled with a frightened squawk. Next instant von Dietz cried, 'All right … *follow me!*' and flung himself out of the door into the storm. The impossible adventure had commenced.

CHAPTER 7

The sunken road ran straight to the sea, some two metres lower than the surrounding fields. It was the ideal escape route, von Dietz told himself, as his men scrambled down the steep bank into it, ducking occasionally when a blinding flash of lightning lit up the scene, but with the raging storm covering their escape from the houses.

To the right, he could see the explosions of the Soviet shells as the enemy attempted to stop the Third Battalion's attack. Von Dietz nodded his head in approval. The Third was playing it exactly right. The Russian artillery barrage would delay even further any attempt on the part of their infantry to the front of the guns discovering that the attack was a feint and would be broken off as soon as the force retreating from the coastal town joined up with the Third.

'Everybody's on the road, sir!' Bulle called nervously from below, the raindrops erupting in white fury on his helmet.

'Excellent.' Von Dietz dropped to the road. 'Off we go!'

Bent double against the wind, the raindrops lashing their faces cruelly, the wind buffeting their skinny bodies and whipping their uniforms tightly about them, they set off, each man tense and apprehensive, for if they were spotted now, it would mean death. Caught on the road in the complete open with no cover, they'd be sitting ducks.

They struggled on, each soldier immersed in his own thoughts, wrapped in a cocoon of raging wind and savage rain. There was always a sense of unreality about battle, a strange dreamlike quality, until actual combat occurred and you were lost in the atavistic primitive butchery; but never had von Dietz experienced its strangeness in the way he did now. For nature itself rivalled the fury of the pounding guns and the howl of the shrapnel when the shells exploded, as if some God on high wanted to show mankind just how puny it was in comparison with the power of the elements.

Time passed. Von Dietz told himself they were getting closer to the point where they would link up with the Third Battalion. Bulle at one point stumbled over a body of one of their own wounded. He was one of the party which had gone with the Pill and obviously had not been able to make it. Now he lay sprawled in the mud, sightless eyes staring into nothing, mouth opened stupidly, the rain running down his glazed ashen face in a myriad cold tears. Hastily von Dietz bent down and closed the eyelids, then passed on.

The Soviet bombardment now started to straddle both sides of the sunken road. The men bent even more as the Stalin organs exploded in great screeching shattering sounds, splattering them with mud and gravel, threatening to engulf everything in their life-destroying fury. A soldier just to von Dietz's front ducked too late as a great glowing fist-sized chunk of steel hissed through the air. He did not even have time to give one last scream. The steel sliced neatly through his neck and while the headless torso seemed to remain standing for a long time, the severed head, complete with helmet, rolled like a ball to von Dietz's feet, the shocked eyes staring up at the horrified officer, as if in accusation. He fought back the hot sour vomit that flooded his throat and stepping over it, hurried on.

Five minutes later they were through the barrage and crawling cautiously up the rain-soaked embankment, shivering with the sudden cold that came from the storm-lashed sea, limbs like ice, shaking their heads to prevent the rain dripping from their helmets from blinding them.

Before them the Third Battalion had gone to ground, little groups of grey-clad figures dug in in shallow pits everywhere, cowering before the Soviet fire, raising themselves for a fleeting instant, firing and then ducking back under cover once more.

Von Dietz nodded his approval. The Third had done well. There were not many dead lying around and the commander's dispositions meant that the Battalion could disengage from the enemy without too much trouble.

'The rest of you remain here,' he commanded. 'When the Third breaks off action and retreats to the road, you'll keep up the volume of fire so that Friend Ivan doesn't realize what's going on. Clear?'

They nodded their heads, their faces very sombre. They all knew just how risky this whole business was.

'And for God's sake, don't shoot our own people,' he added, more as a mild joke than a warning. But his sally raised no smiles. He shrugged and wriggled over the top.

Five minutes later he was relaying his instructions to the young captain now commanding the Third Battalion since its commander had been killed. He was young and tense, but capable and understood fully the difficulty of the situation. 'We'll do it, sir, don't worry,' he announced confidently enough.

'Of course,' von Dietz echoed slapping him on the shoulder, 'of course, you will! Any wounded?'

'Just walking wounded, sir. They won't hinder us.'

'Excellent. By the way did you see Pill — I mean the MO with his group,' von Dietz added, as the Third prepared to move back.

'No, sir.'

'I expect he'll have continued along the sunken road without contacting you. It would be the safest thing to do,' he said dismissing his old friend from his mind. 'All right, Captain, let's get this thing on the road. *Move 'em!*'

Now the Third Battalion started to slip out of their positions in platoon groups, relief clear on the men's faces as they stole back, crouched low, springing in and out of the new, steaming shell-holes, taking casualties all the time from the Russian artillery, but getting ever closer to the cover of the sunken road.

Von Dietz saw a greenbeak hit in the back of the head. Unlike the old heads, he had not pulled his helmet down to cover that spot, the way old heads did when they were retreating. The entry wound was a small red hole; the exit was a great exploding red monstrosity. His features slid down his face in a revolting red slurry like melting candle-wax. Another white-haired boy ran screaming past him, his eye blasted out. An old head went down to his front, shot in the groin, moaning pitifully, writhing back and forth until von Dietz took careful aim with one of his last slugs and blasted him into eternity; it was the merciful thing to do.

And then what was left of the Third Battalion was under cover, and gasping like ancient asthmatics they hurried away from that scene of carnage, heading for the unknown. What was left of the 69th Regiment was coming out. The rain continued to pound down...

The Russian dead lay everywhere, entangled on the wire, sprawled in the road, two crouched there as if still alive, and talking. Perhaps one had just been in the act of saying, 'keep your turnip down,' when the German bullets had struck them both. Now all of them gave off the odour of camembert and crawled with maggots.

The Pill bit his bottom lip. They were not a pleasant spectacle and he could see the effect the sight was having on his wounded. 'Come on, boys,' he urged, 'speed it up! They're only stiffs you know.' He picked up a stone and flung it at the great black glistening crow feasting on the eyes of a corpse hanging on the barbed wire like a bundle of old rags. Sullenly the overfed bird fluttered to the safety of one of the skeletal trees now fringing the escape route. He shuddered and passed on.

Now the thunder of the artillery had died away considerably, muted by the steady hiss of the rain.

The Pill bringing up the rear of the little column calculated they might be some two or three kilometres behind the Russian line. It would be wise to keep the wounded going as quickly as possible until they were directly behind it. There they would wait for the main body of fighting men to catch up with them and be rested for that final, highly dangerous business of forcing the Russian line. 'At least we'll have surprise on our side,' he told himself, talking to himself in the fashion of all lonely men; for as MO he could relate his worries and fears to no one save Horst. He knew he had to be hard and keep his thoughts to himself. It was not a matter of callousness, but the exigencies of war. How often had he felt the poignant loss of some man he had served with and had liked, but had forced himself to plunge back into the activities of the present, letting new men take their place so that life could go on. Life! he told himself, *death* would be a better word. For a few moments he thought of all those broken bodies that had passed through his hands in these last terrible years. His nightmares were full of them, of him working against time, severed limbs piled up knee-high around him, slashing, sawing, cutting … limb after limb.

He shook his head suddenly. To the right front something had moved. In an instant he was alert, his nerves tingling electrically. He opened his mouth to call a warning to the corporal with the shattered right arm who was leading the column. Too late!

Abruptly the wood to their front was full of dark running figures. A tommy gun chattered. The corporal's head shattered like that of a wax dummy hit by a hammer. Blood and fragments of bone flew everywhere.

'*Partisans!… Partisans!*' one of the wounded screamed hysterically, as the civilians came skidding and sliding down the rain-slick embankment onto the sunken road.

A medical orderly, raised his satchel with its bold red cross, 'Don't shoot … don't shoot!' he cried. 'Doctor … hosp —' His plea ended in a howl of absolute agony, as a blast of slugs at short range slammed his body against the embankment. He trailed down it slowly, arms extended, as if he were crucified, bright red blood jetting from a dozen wounds across his chest. A Russian ran at a wounded soldier who had sat down, holding up his bandaged arms in surrender. He kicked the screaming man in the face. The German's neck clicked back, his spine broken. He was dead before he hit the ground. His face contorted with horror, as the Russians started slaughtering the men at the head of the column with systematic savage cruelty, the Pill doubled forward, thrusting aside his terrified wounded who cowered there awaiting their fate like dumb animals.

'*Doktor!*' he screamed fervently. '*Doktor* … we surrender!' He pushed aside a soldier who knelt there, head bent, praying frantically, and came face to face with a bearded giant, his yellow face pocked with deep pits.

The Russian raised the red hatchet he bore in his ham like fist and then taking in the stars on the Pill's shoulders and the red cross armband on his sleeve brought it down. 'You Fritz doctor?' he asked in broken German, revealing a mouthful of stainless steel teeth, as if he was proud of them and ready to display them on every possible occasion.

'Yes, yes, *doctor!*' Pill screamed, seizing on the word, as if it meant life itself. 'Stop your men… *Please!*' He clutched the giant's paw desperately, as to his right, a Russian placed his muddy boot on the skinny chest of a wounded man he had just bayoneted and dragged out his gleaming red blade with that familiar sucking noise.

The giant shook his head and now the Pill could see the infinite evil in the partisan's eyes; he knew with the clarity of a sudden vision that he could expect no mercy from him. Now it was his fate to die here on this God-forsaken, nameless Russian road. He let his shoulders slump in resignation as the bloody slaughter continued all around him in the mud.

'Where rest of Fritzes?' the partisan asked, raising his hatchet with the bright red gleaming blade. 'Come after you?'

With one final effort, telling himself that his death might yet serve some purpose, the Pill cried, 'No, no, they're going to sea! To the beaches!'

The partisan shouted something in Russian. A couple of his followers broke off the slaughter and started to scramble up the muddy bank, slinging their weapons as they disappeared over the edge; and then the blade descended. The Pill felt an overwhelming, all-consuming pain explode inside his skull. Red waves swamped him. 'Horst —' he whispered, as the blood streamed down his shattered face, and his crumpled body sunk to the rain-soaked ground. Hastily the partisan leader started to loot it…

'My God … it's Pill!' Von Dietz broke through the group of soaked, silent men staring down at the victims of the massacre lying there in their sodden bandages, the rain beating down on their still contorted bodies mercilessly. Carefully he turned the body, trying to ignore the great gaping wound at the side of his head.

The old man's face had already turned that waxen yellow, which always made the dead appear as meaningless as tailor's dummies in a store-window. The eyes were glassy and half-open and his lips were bared to reveal teeth gritted in his last agony. Slowly, very slowly von Dietz reached out and slipped the eyelids down to cover that gaze for ever. 'Why did the fiends kill the wounded?' someone asked. 'They could have let them surrender. They wouldn't have done anyone any harm.'

'*Why*?' Von Dietz asked himself as he knelt there with the raindrops streaming from his bent helmet. 'Why did Pill have to die? Or any of them for that matter? What was the purpose of their sacrifice? Would anything come of their cruel deaths? *WHY*?'

It was that overwhelming question that front swine always asked themselves when a friend died like this; and as always there was no answer to it. Reluctantly he raised himself and touched his hand to his streaming helmet in a last salute. They had come a long way together. Now the road had come to an end. He would have liked to have buried him, but there was no time. 'Good-bye, Pill,' he whispered, the grey rain drops rolling down his skinny cheeks like cold tears. 'Bye…'

Two hours later they burst through the surprised Russian line and were streaming westwards to their own positions before the Russians were aware of what had happened. Collapsing in the mud of the trenches, silent and morose, drained of all energy, they were spent useless men. The Pill's final sacrifice had not been in vain; they had survived another day...

CHAPTER 8

'*Winkelmann!*' the Bull called out standing there in the dripping rain in front of the shabby parade, 'has anyone seen Winkelmann?'

'Yes, Sarnt-Major,' Deltgen called back angrily, hating this customary roll-call after battle as a kind of profit-and-loss balancing of the books for the rear-echelon stallions of the staff, 'he's dead, the silly bastard.'

The Bull glared at him. 'Are you sure?'

'Of course, I'm shitting well sure! He got his stupid turnip shot off by a Stalin Organ.'

Dutifully Sergeant-Major Bulle ticked off the dead man's name on the regimental roll and continued: 'Witing?' he called, voice muffled by the rain. And that litany of death went on.

On the fringes of the parade, cooks, temporary details and the usual rear-line flotsam watched them from the cover of the huts, some with looks of sympathy on their faces, others with looks of bewilderment; for there was a gulf between these silent, hard-eyed men who had just returned from the Front and themselves. They were front swine; and front swine were a breed of their own.

Von Dietz watched too, seeing the ghosts of dead men in the appalling gaps in their tired ranks, knowing now that the Regiment would never be the same; the bloodletting had been too great. They would march again admittedly, but now their minds would always look backwards to the ones who had been killed and could never be replaced. Finally Bulle was finished. He stood the men at ease and with no attempt at his former swagger, limped through the puddles to a waiting von Dietz to make his report. The CO waiting there, limp shoulders bowed with weariness, heard his report as if it were coming from a great distance. Automatically he touched his hand to his battered, soaked cap and said, 'Dismiss the men.'

'Yessir.'

A minute later the survivors started to stagger off to find shelter, food and sleep, each man haggard and drawn, glassy-eyed with exhaustion, stumbling through the rain, as if they were dream-walking. In awed silence, the watchers made way for these weary front swine, who only wished to fling themselves down somewhere, gnaw a crust of bread in silence, then sleep, sleep, sleep until they had recovered their nerve.

But that was not to be. Even as the Russian guns started to rumble once more indicating that the enemy was not just going to defend his line, but was preparing for a further attack, a long grey familiar Mercedes started to nose its way through the puddles into the tumbledown village. Automatically with the last of their strength, the surviving officers and NCOs halted their men and made them come to some semblance of attention. It was General Degenhardt, accompanied by Colonel Kraemer, both of them radiating confidence and good-living, as they saluted to left and right with crisp military efficiency.

The sullenness of the survivors was clear. It was expressed on every face, as the car rolled past; for now the men of the 69th had learnt from their two sister regiments that Degenhardt had been prepared to sacrifice them to the Russians. After all they had suffered, his surprise appearance seemed the final indignity. Here and there men began to mutter angrily. Others hawked and spat defiantly in the path of the Mercedes. Red Rudi, the ex-communist, as angry as ever shook his fist at the car and bent down as if he were looking for a stone to cast at it. Magically all tiredness had fled to be replaced by a vital burning anger. The onlookers sensed it and as General Degenhardt's car finally came to a halt opposite Colonel von Dietz, they drew back as men do outside a tavern when a fight is in the offing. The damp air was suddenly heavy with tension.

As the two of them stepped stiffly from the open Mercedes, General von Degenhardt seemed oblivious to the tension, and if Colonel Kraemer sensed it, his hard overbearing face gave no indication.

Degenhardt, followed a little to the right by Kraemer, ploughed through the mud, a stupid smile still on his fat face.

Von Dietz's was stony, revealing no emotion whatsoever, save that a vein ticked nervously at his temple and anyone watching him closely could have seen his clenched fist, its knuckles white with suppressed anger.

Degenhardt halted five paces away and waited. Nothing happened. Von Dietz stood there unmoving, eyes icy.

The smile started to fade from General Degenhardt's face. To his right Kraemer gave a severe official frown. He looked as if he were making a mental note of this military discourtesy, which would be remarked on later. 'Congratulations for having brought it off so well — under the circumstances, Colonel von Dietz,' Degenhardt blustered, still unaware of the ominous mutterings of the men all around him. 'No one but the 69th could have done it…'

His voice trailed away to nothing. Von Dietz's hand had fallen slowly to the Russian pistol he had taken from one of their dead and thrust into his belt. The gesture was unmistakably threatening.

Kraemer broke in. 'We've got some good news for you, von Dietz.' He paused momentarily. There was no reaction from the ragged, mud-stained von Dietz with his hand clasped to the pistol butt. 'Corps is pulling the 69th out. Your Regiment will return to Germany for rest and refit — the rest of the Division will follow later.' He forced a fake smile. 'I think that is a piece of very welcome information, don't you?'

'I agree,' Degenhardt said, recovering his confidence. 'It'll probably be Sennalager. All very quiet up there. Plenty of good beer and women. Your men will —'

'Why did you abandon us?' von Dietz spoke for the first time, his voice harsh and bitter, blue eyes like ice.

'*Abandon you?*' Degenhardt blustered. 'What are you talking about, von Dietz?'

'You know!' Von Dietz's hand tightened even more on the pistol. All round him the muttering of his men grew ever louder. 'You left us to our fate. If it had not been for the courage of my men, we would have been massacred.' Kraemer's fake smile vanished. 'Have a care, Colonel,' he snapped. 'You are talking to your senior divisional officer, you know. I know that you and your men have been through a bad time —' He stopped short, the courage draining visibly from his face, his cheeks suddenly pale and bloodless.

Von Dietz had drawn his pistol, his teeth bared wolfishly. Slowly he clicked back the hammer and as if mesmerized, Kraemer could see his forefinger knuckle whiten as he took first pressure.

'What the devil are you going to do?' Kraemer hissed, reefing back. Next to him Degenhardt raised his pudgy hands to protect his face instinctively, as if he half-expected a bullet to come his way at any moment.

'Go,' von Dietz whispered. 'Go ... *now*! Or else...'

'You damn fool, von Dietz!' Kraemer cried, as Degenhardt backed off, hands still held protectively in front of his fat body, 'you can't get away with this! This is the German Army! I know what you have been through —'

'GO!' von Dietz bellowed, exasperated beyond all bounds. 'BEFORE IT'S TOO LATE!'

But it was already too late for Degenhardt and Kraemer. Something snapped in the men of the 69th, a kind of collective madness overcame them. A stone flew through the air. Behind the two retreating men, the windscreen of the Mercedes shattered. The driver, showered with broken glass, took one look at the crazy contorted animal faces of the mob advancing on him and flung himself from the seat, to dash for safety before it was too late. A low hum started to come from the survivors, growing in intensity by the second. Kraemer and Degenhardt backed against the side of the Mercedes, faces wild with fear. Kraemer fumbled for his pistol. 'Get back,' he cried, 'get back, you mad dogs…' He howled with pain as another rock sailed through the air and smashed against the side of his face. He let the pistol drop.

Now it was Degenhardt's turn. He grabbed for his pistol. In a frenzy of fear, he screamed, '*I'll shoot the first man* —' and pulled the trigger. To his immediate front, a soldier's face erupted into a startling, flowing gore, as if someone had just thrown a handful of strawberry jam at it.

The crowd roared and surged forward. No emotion visible on his face, von Dietz watched as the two officers were submerged by the throng, low obscene primeval cries coming from their enraged throats, as they kicked and punched, stabbed and hacked. Until finally it was over and all that was left was the bloody bundles pressed deep into the black mud. Degenhardt and Kraemer were dead. They had paid the price for their treachery.

Frozen as if for eternity, Colonel von Dietz watched the 69th as they began to disperse, their heads hanging, as if suddenly ashamed, not looking at the men they had slaughtered, brushing by the gaping rear-echelon stallions. He knew a terrible crime had been committed and that all of them would have to pay for it one day sooner or later, but somehow he could not be shocked by it. It seemed that he was in an entirely different world looking down from another planet at a weird, uncanny marionette show, which bore no relationship to his own private world.

Then as to the east the Russian barrage grew in ever-increasing fury, he turned and wandered off, all anger gone from his face, even smiling a little...

But Colonel von Dietz and what was left of his Regiment were not fated to pay the price of their terrible crime that particular spring. Twenty-four hours after they had murdered General Degenhardt and his Chief-of-Staff, the whole division had begun to retreat before the massive Soviet attack on the Leningrad Front. Division was followed by Corps and then by all corps. The tragedy of the Northern Sector had commenced. Hundreds of thousands of field-greys fought against annihilation as the red tide of the enemy swept all before it. Corps were reduced to divisions, divisions to regiments, regiments to battalions, battalions to companies. Now all order vanished. It was a matter of *sauve qui peut*.

Transport blocked all roads to the west and safety as the Russians advanced relentlessly, losing thousands dead and wounded, but spurred on by the sweet scent of victory after so many months of defeat. Vast depots went up in flames and soon the transport followed; what was the use of trucks now? The soldiers took to the countryside, tossing away their equipment progressively as they became ever more weary. Now the Red Cossacks trailed them across those soaked, limitless plains by their abandoned gas-masks, ground-sheets, machine-guns, even rifles.

Northern Russia became the burial ground of Hitler's hopes, as the isolated bands of field-grey uniform, lousy, starving, unspeakably filthy, slouched westwards, shoulders sagging, only capable of new energy when the lookout cried that dread warning, 'Cossacks … *Cossacks on the horizon!*'

Now soldiers started to surrender by the platoon, company, battalion! Like motors that had run out of fuel, they would let their emaciated debilitated bodies slump down into the wet grass, heads sunk and hopelessly wait for the inevitable — the knouts lashed across their narrow shoulders, the curved gleaming sabre cleaving down on their shaven skulls. THE END!

Only the toughest of the front swine survived; and they survived by cunning, loyalty to each other, and naked brutality. Men from other units were slaughtered for the sake of their rations — without compunction. The Russians were tricked time and time again. Stragglers were kept going by threats, pleas, blows. On the old heads staggered, the skin hanging in folds on their wind-burnt, unshaven faces, eyes bulging from their starved features, the spring rains soaking their ragged uniforms through the holes of which their ribs showed. On and on, their progress marked by little mounds of soil and rocks from which a boot or hand protruded to remind those who followed that this had once been a man.

And then it was over. The line was stabilized again and the pursuit petered out. Like grey ghosts the survivors and stragglers came reeling in to be stared at by the fresh troops defending the new line. General Lindemann's Army had vanished. Never again would Germany's might threaten Leningrad. It was all over. Only a few thousand ragged scarecrows were left of that great confident army, once three hundred thousand strong.

Colonel von Dietz brought in what was left of the 69th on the afternoon of 20th April 1943. It was Hitler's birthday. Back in the Reich and in the rear areas, they would be celebrating the Führer's birthday with speeches, parades, parties.

But here out on the dripping wet steppe there was nothing to celebrate. Death and destruction stretched to the very horizon. Shattered vehicles, blackened and tangled heaps of wreckage, were everywhere. Upturned rifles like dead, withered stalks marked the dead. Over the kilometres of rusting barbed wire hung the bodies of the last to die in a ghastly and infinite tableau. Dead lay piled in the pits, with here and there a skeletal hand reaching up as if in supplication and a pair of eyes staring up accusingly from a skull already beginning to rot. There was nothing to celebrate about this gigantic desolation which marked the defeat of Hitler's hopes for a victory in the north.

The survivors ate in silence, broken only by the mournful drip-drip of the rain from the ruined trees and slide of the blades of shovel against gravel as the burial parties dug the mass graves.

Colonel von Dietz squalled with them, seeing faces which were no longer there — von Doerr, Sanders, Dietrich, the Pill, a host of them, pale, staring unspeaking — telling himself that they, the dead, would march with them for ever until they were all dead. Now he felt the pain of that loss only dully; the horrors of these last weeks had numbed his senses.

It was perhaps an hour later that the ancient, wood-burning trucks started to rattle up through the mud, to bear them to the railhead to start their long journey back to the Reich, two thousand kilometres away. Without a command being spoken, the men started to form up wearily in order to climb aboard.

Von Dietz waited till finally they had shuffled to some sort of order under the shocked gazes of the middle-aged rear-echelon swine who were going to drive them. 'Soldiers of the 69th, Comrades,' he broke the heavy brooding silence, his voice low but powerful, as he gazed around their gaunt, hollowed-out faces. 'We are going home. You have fought the good fight. You deserve the rest. But remember that you have an obligation now — *to our dead*!' His own lean face was abruptly animated with a trace of the old fierceness in his cold grey eyes. 'Don't forget them, never *dare* to forget them! They died so you could live to become front swine...' His voice broke; he could say no more. Without another word, he walked to his truck.

Slowly, sadly the survivors started to clamber aboard the trucks. Doors slammed. Drivers started their engines. The damp air was full of the stink of wood gas. Men slumped on the straw, their eyes closed.

One by one the trucks began to move out, jolting over the rough road, leaving that scene of desolation, that great rubbish-heap of metal and human flesh — the Front — behind them. No one looked back. The front swine were going home...

A NOTE TO THE READER

Dear Reader,
If you have enjoyed this novel enough to leave a review on **Amazon** and **Goodreads**, then we would be truly grateful.
Sapere Books

Sapere Books is an exciting new publisher of brilliant fiction and popular history.

To find out more about our latest releases and our monthly bargain books visit our website: **saperebooks.com**

www.ingramcontent.com/pod-product-compliance
Lightning Source LLC
Chambersburg PA
CBHW060433180626
46817CB00007B/2795